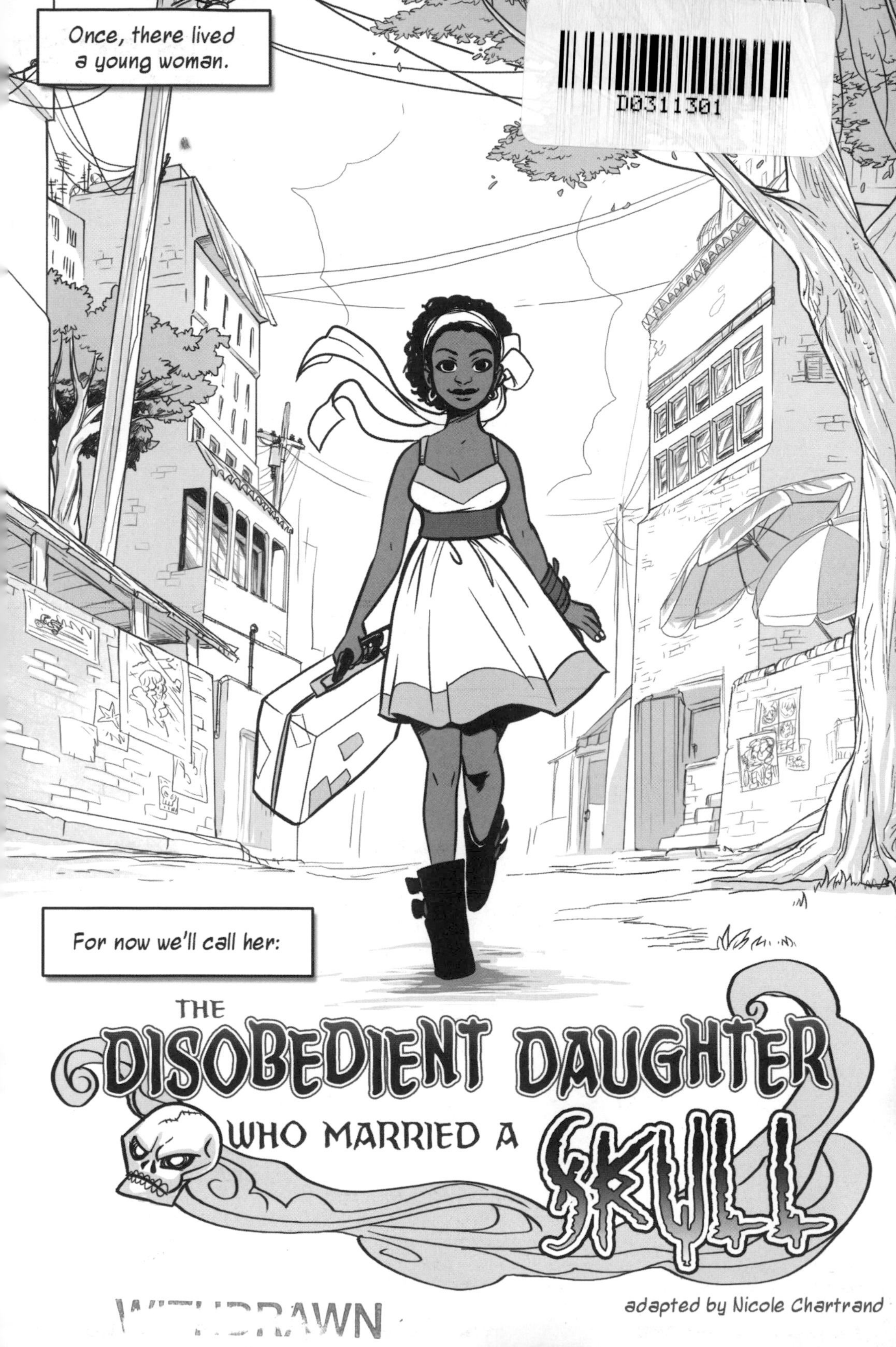
Once, there lived a young woman.
For now we'll call her:
THE DISOBEDIENT DAUGHTER WHO MARRIED A SKULL
adapted by Nicole Chartrand

She was known as the most beautiful girl in town (but also the most stubborn).
She turned heads wherever she went...
Siiigh
?!
HEY, YOU CAN'T IMPROVE PERFECTION!
Okay, so maybe she was a little bit vain, too.

THE GIRL WHO MARRIED A SKULL

AND OTHER AFRICAN STORIES

A CAUTIONARY FABLES + FAIRYTALES BOOK

editors
C. Spike Trotman, Kate Ashwin, Kel McDonald, Taneka Stotts

cover art
Becky Dreistadt

book design
Matt Sheridan

print technician
Rhiannon Rasmussen-Silverstein

Publisher's Cataloging-In-Publication Data
(Prepared by The Donohue Group, Inc.)

Names: Ashwin, Kate, editor. | McDonald, Kel, editor. | Trotman, Charlie Spike, 1978- editor.
Title: The girl who married a skull, and other African stories : a cautionary fables & fairytales book / [editors, Kate Ashwin, Kel McDonald, and Charlie Spike Trotman].
Description: Iron Circus Comics edition. | [Chicago, Illinois] : Iron Circus Comics, [2018] | Previously published in 2014 as: A cautionary fables & fairytales book. | Interest age level: 010-013. | Summary: "An anthology of African folktales playfully interpreted by modern cartoonists."--Provided by publisher.
Identifiers: ISBN 9781945820243
Subjects: LCSH: Fables, African--Comic books, strips, etc. | Fairy tales--Africa--Comic books, strips, etc. | Africans--Folklore--Comic books, strips, etc. | CYAC: Fables, African--Cartoons and comics. | Fairy tales--Africa--Cartoons and comics. | Africans--Folklore--Cartoons and comics. | LCGFT: Fables. | Fairy tales. | Graphic novels.
Classification: LCC PZ7.7 .G57 2018 | DDC [Fic] 398.20967--dc23

inquiry@ironcircus.com www.ironcircus.com

s t r a n g e   a n d   a m a z i n g

first printing: October 2018 Printed in China ISBN: 978-1-945820-24-3

While her parents begged her to choose a husband among her admirers and settle down.
I THINK I'D RATHER TRAVEL OR SOMETHING...
Their daughter paid them no mind.
Little did they know that word of her beauty (perhaps also of her stubbornness) had travelled past the borders of the human world...
I MUST HAVE HER AS MY WIFE!!
HELLO?
HEY, IT'S ME. GET THE BOYS, I HAVE A FEW FAVORS TO ASK YOU.
HOW ARE YOU EVEN USING THAT PHONE??
...and that her newest suitor had hatched a nefarious plan to win her hand.

A short time later:
AHEM!
I MUST HAV-- I MEAN, I LOVE YOU! I WANT TO SWEEP YOU OFF YOUR FEET AND VISIT EXOTIC PLACES TOGETHER!
HELLLLOOOOO!
SO, MARRY ME! ... ALSO, HELLO!
A mysterious man from a faraway land made her an offer she couldn't refuse.

Almost as quickly, they left together for the exotic place that he called home.

This is where things start to get a little weird.

?!
TUG
BEWARE!
JUST MARRIED
NOWHERE
(YOU ARE HE
LAND OF TH
Cool
LAND O
HE LIVING
DON'T
TURN BACK
ABANDON HOPE!
(BRING LUNCH!)

As soon as they set foot over the border, the girl could tell that something was wrong.

SO... UM... ER... HONEY, HOW FAR IS YOUR HOME FROM HERE?
TOO CLOSE NOW TO TURN BACK, WIFE.
AHEM.
SORRY, BRO,
BUT CAN YOU GIVE ME BACK MY LEG YET?
OF COURSE.
?!
TWIST!
HERE, THANKS FOR LETTING ME BORROW IT, MAN.
SURE.
!!!
POP!

Before she could wrap her head around what had happened, monsters had surrounded them, demanding that her husband return his borrowed body...

FOOT!
EYES!
SKIN!
EARS!
SPLEEENN!!!
ARM!
BACKBONE!

...piece by piece...

...until there was nothing left but a skull at her feet.
UMAAAAAAAAAAAAAAUGHOKAY THIS ISN'T WORKING OUT SORRY BUT RELATIONSHIPS BASED ON PH-PH-PHYSICAL ATTRACTION RARELY LAST SO UH SORRY IT'S NOT Y-YOU IT'S DEFINITELY ME AND I REALLY HAVE TO GO BACK NOW I LEFT MY HAIR IN THE OVEN AND MY FAVOURITE TOOTHBRUSH IS STILL--
I TOLD YOU, WIFE. IT'S TOO FAR FOR YOU TO GO BACK ALONE.
A MERE HUMAN CAN'T CROSS THE BORDER OUT OF THE LAND OF THE DEAD ON THEIR OWN. SO THERE'S NOTHING YOU CAN DO...
...EXCEPT COME HOME WITH ME AND BE A GOOD, OBEDIENT WIFE.
GULP
The skull's home was a small, ancient hut, where he lived (if you can call it that) with his mother.
MA, I'M HOME! I WENT TO THE HUMAN WORLD AND BROUGHT BACK A WIFE!
zzzZzzzZ-- A... WHAT?

A REAL LIVE HUMAN WIFE! SHE'S GONNA COOK AND STUFF--

A HUMAN WIFE?! COOKING?! SON, YOU'RE A SKULL YOU DON'T EVEN EAT! HOW MANY TIMES HAVE I--

zzzZZZzz

WHUMP

The skull's mother was a tiny woman, so old that she spent most of her time fast asleep.

ARE YOU ALRIGHT, MA'AM?

But she seemed nice enough, so the girl was glad to help her up and to get her some tea.

THERE'S NOTHING THEY LIKE MORE THAN FEASTING ON HUMAN FLESH.
WHAT TIME IS IT?!
GORGING THEMSELVES ON BRAINS AND ALL THAT. IT'S A RARE TREAT FOR THEM.
SO, SORRY, I GUESS.
WHY DID YOU NOT TELL ME THIS?!
I FORGOT!
BESIDES, YOU'LL DO FINE AS A SKULL, PROBABLY. I DON'T REALLY CARE.
WHY DID YOU MARRY ME IF YOU DIDN'T CARE!?
BECAUSE YOU WERE CUTE. WHY'D YOU MARRY ME?
BECAU--UGH!! THERE'S GOT TO BE SOME WAY I CAN GET BACK HOME BEFORE SUNSET!!
Luckily for her, the skull's mother was not an ordinary human, but a witch.
Moved by the girl's plight (or maybe just eager to get her out of the house to bring the decibel level back down), she offered to help.
She cast a spell calling forth a gentle breeze to carry the girl home to the human world.

KNOCK
KNOCK

Of course, it wasn't going to be that easy.

SLAM
ZZZZZZ
ZZZZ
The first wind that came calling was not quite gentle enough for her to ride home.
WAHAHAHA
ZZZZZZ

KNOCK
KNOCK

THAT MUST BE IT!! THANKS FOR EVERYTHI--

AAAAH
And the skull also neglected to mention that the many monstrous denizens of the Land of the Dead often liked to have their dinners early.

NOT THE WIND, HUH?

NO.
MA...? WAKE UP!

BAM

ZZZZ
ZZZ
OH, OOPS! HMM, JUST... KEEP THEM BUSY FOR A MOMENT, DEAR AND I'LL CALL A NICER WIND TO COME GET YOU.

"KEEP THEM BUSY"?!
BAM
BAM
BAM
BAM
BAM
HOW AM I SUPPOSED TO... HMMM.

WHAT ARE YOU LOOKING AT? NO.

OK, GOT MY SCARF... NOW WHERE'D I PUT MY PERFUME...?
NO MATTER WHAT YOU'RE PLANNING, THE ANSWER IS NO!

THOSE MONSTERS CAN SMELL HUMANS. THAT'S WHY THEY'RE HERE, RIGHT?
LOOK, JUST TAKE MY SCARF WITH SOME OF MY PERFUME OUT THERE AND SAY I'M GONE--

--OR ALREADY EATEN-- AND THAT THE SCARF IS ALL THAT'S LEFT OF ME!
I DON'T FEEL LIKE IT.

Pouf
Pouf

THROW

I HATE YOOOOOUUUU!!!!
WAS THAT THE HUMAN?

OW! UGH! -SIGH-
THE GIRL WANTS ME TO TELL YOU SHE'S ALREADY BEEN DEVOURED.
BOP!
THIS SMELLY SCARF IS ALL THAT'S LEFT OF HER, YOU CAN GO NOW.

...
IT SMELLS LIKE HUMAN.
YOU SMELL LIKE HUMAN.

GIVE US THE TASTY HUMAN!

THE BREEZE IS WAITING FOR YOU, DEARIE.
TIME FOR YOU TO GO BACK HOME!
RIGHT! THANK Y--
NOW YOU'LL BE GOOD AND LISTEN TO *EVERYTHING* YOUR PARENTS SAY, *WON'T YOU?*
OR ELSE?!
I--

WHOOSH
LET'S GET OUT OF HERE, BREEZY!
CAN I CALL YOU BREEZY?

THANKS AGAIN FOR HELPING ME!!

NO HARD FEELINGS, RIGHT?

YOU WERE A ROTTEN WIFE ANYWAY!!

And with that, she started her journey back to the human world, and her family. Or something.
AND THAT'S THE STORY OF HOW I ENDED UP HERE!
NOW IF YOU DON'T MIND LENDING ME A HAND, I MIGHT NEED A LITTLE HELP GETTING DOWN.
OK.
I'M AFIONG BY THE WAY.
I'M UCHE...
OH, AND THAT'S BREEZY OVER THERE.
HE'S STUCK TOO, IF YOU CAN HELP HIM.
...OK.

Shortly thereafter...

...UCHE, CAN I ASK YOU SOMETHING?

SURE?

DO YOU LIKE TO TRAVEL?

NOW!! GRAND OPENING SPECIAL!

Gentle Breeze Deliveries

Our couriers ride like the wind!
Ask about our Special Grand Opening Rates!
for inquiries call Afiong or Uche
(Deliveries to the Land of the Dead only during daylight hours)

The end.

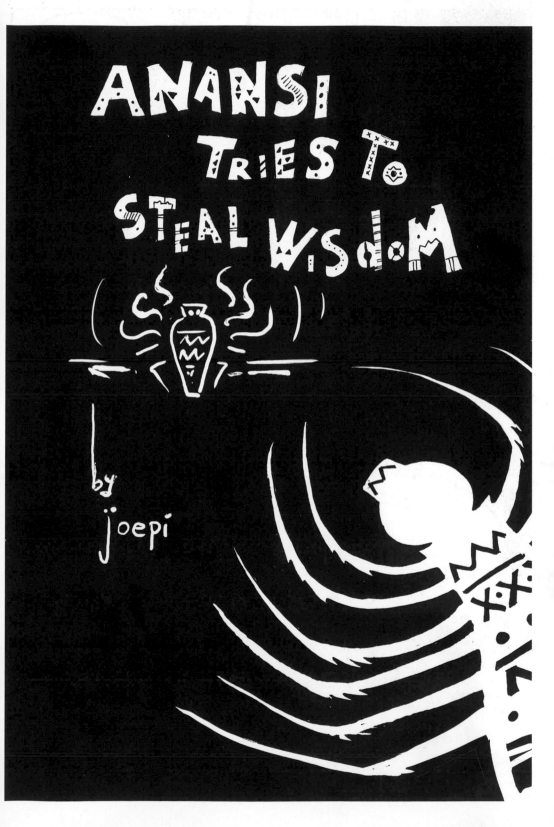

ANANSI TRIES TO STEAL WISDOM

by joepi

Anansi was incredibly smart.
... He invented toys.

clap
clap clap!
clap!
clap!
clap! clap!
clap!
He danced.
clap!
clap!
clap!
clap!
clap!
clap!
clap!

He also knew about language.
Thanks to the redundancy of language yxx cxn stxll xndxrstxnd whxt x xm wrxtxng xvxn xf x rxplxcx xll thx vxwxls wxth xn "x."
(t gts lttl hrdr f y dn't vn knw whr th vwls r)*
I was walking in the park and this guy waved at me. Then he said, "I'm sorry, I thought you were someone else."
I said "I am." **
Never odd or even.
With his sixteen limbs he could do anything.
*Steven Pinker ** Demitri Martin

On one specific day, the wise elder Elephant saw him.
--the biggest planet comes right after the asteroid belt.
Mercury and Venus have no moons.
Atoms are made of electrons, protons, and neutrons.
Anansi, you are VERY smart and VERY talented.
Too bad you're not yet wise.

WHAT!
What do you mean I am not wise?
Wisdom is something good and I can't NOT HAVE something good, sir.
Oh, Anansi, wisdom is like a sunset; it only comes with time.
But--
AND, you can't force it.
but all the BEST and BRILLIANT are wise.
How can I acquire wisdom?
The Elephant said it comes with time.
But I need it NOW, not later.
Why are only old folks the wise ones?

THAT'S IT...
THAT'S IT!!
I can get the wisdom from the elders.
But what if they can't give it away? Or WORSE what if they don't want to give it to me?
They have it. I want it. I'll get it.
Even if I have to steal it.

Later that night.
. . . .
Some of these must have wisdom.

I DO have several limbs.
Time to get more.
So Anansi went...
...from hut to hut...
...of
all
the
elders.

When the night finally came to an end--

--Anansi returned home.

Time to WISE UP!

AJABUL!
Knock
Knock
Knock
Knock

Yes?
Hello, Anansi. I trust your day has started well, yes?
A new day is always a new start, right?
Do you, by any chance happen to know what happened in the village last night?
...No... I don't. Why?
Well, several townsfolk were robbed.

Did you see anything strange or odd?
No, no, no... nothing comes to mind
Well, we shall continue searching. If you find it in you to "share" anything you know,
you can find us at the village.

Oh, no...
they want to
steal MY wisdom.
They know I'm
SMART and
WISE.
I better
hide it.
But where?
!!/ OF COURSE!

UP!

Anansi climbed the tree, but as he almost reached the top...
...he slipped.
SPlat!
OH NO!

ENOUGH
NONESENSE

Anansi! You Ought To Be Ashamed Of Yourself!

You Lied.

You Are Impatient.

You Stole.

You Trespassed.

And Now You Are Being GREEDY And SELFISH.

For This You Will Lose Half Of Your Limbs and Your Hat!
You Will Have More Vision, But No Skills...
...Other Than Crafting Your Own Web.
And You Will Be POISON To Others, So They Will Want You Far Away.
Here, Let Me Help You.

Ever since that day...

...Anansi has searched for the tree where the vase had been broken...

...hoping to ask for forgiveness, and to regain what he had lost.

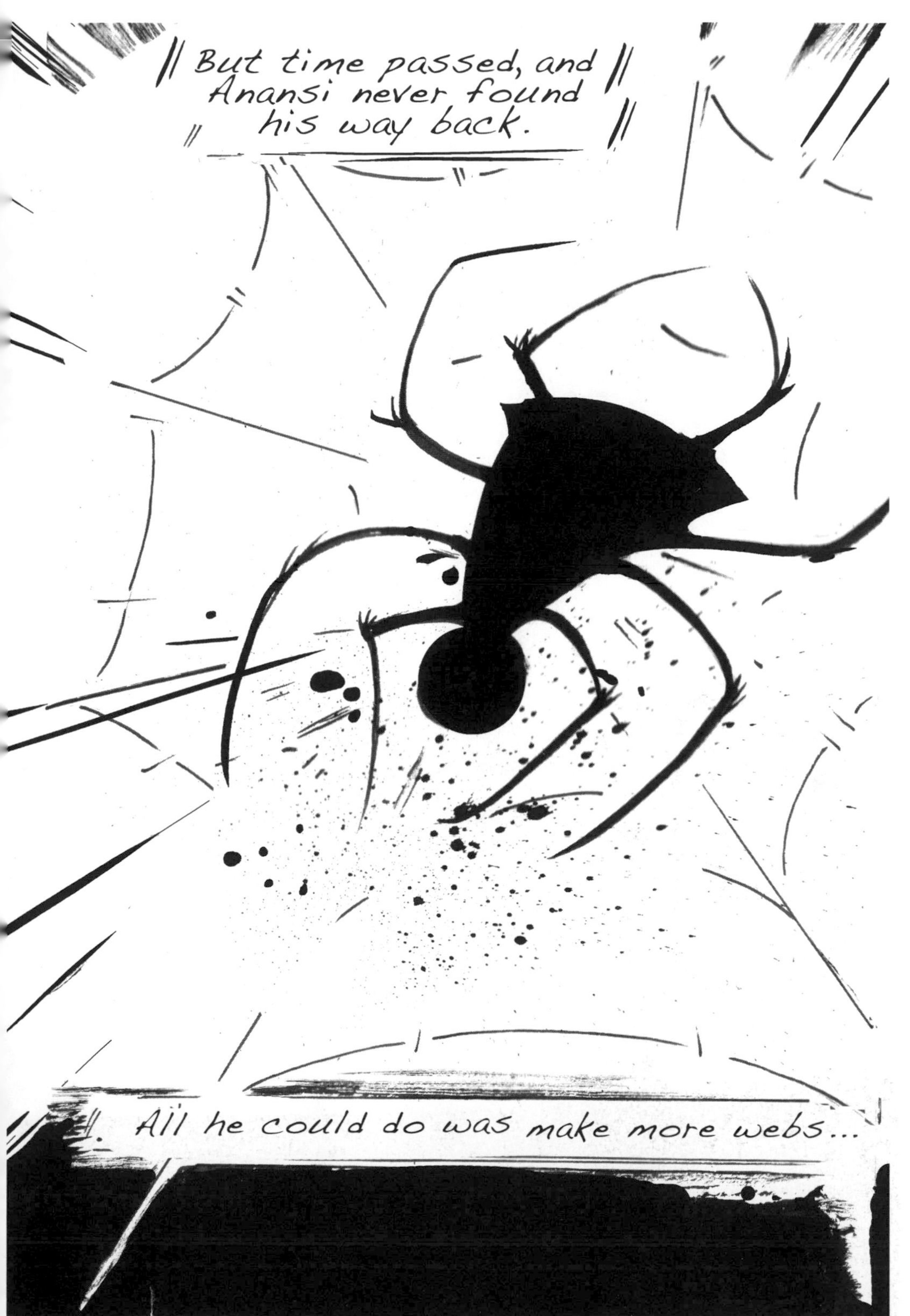
But time passed, and Anansi never found his way back.
All he could do was make more webs...

...and search from tree to tree.

DEMANE AND DEMAZANA
Adapted by Katie and Steven Shanahan
These two orphaned siblings are finally on their own.
Earlier that day, Demane and Demazana decided that they'd had enough of living with their cruel uncle and aunt, and set out to make a new home for themselves.
They left well knowing that the wild was dangerous.
But compared to living with the neglect and abuse from their only remaining family, they chose instead to risk encounters with ferocious beasts, crafty thieves...
...or even...

Cannibals?!

Well, it could just be a rumor, but all the same...

We have to be cautious of any people lurking around.
KNOCK KNOCK

I say we keep this door closed tight and locked at all times.
erf

ESPECIALLY when I'm out hunting.
THUNK

But if I have to let you in, how will I know it's actually you outside?
WIPE
blurp

Uh, well...

WAIT! We could have a secret song!

What?

Hear me out, you'll go...
"I've been hunting all daaaaaaay, and this door blocks my waaaaaaaay. Sister, won't you let me iiiiiiiiiiiiiin."
fwip
And then I'll respond with...
"OKAAAAAAAAY."
Your part sounds a lot easier.

Well you *have* to get the tricky part, because only you can hold those notes so well.
You've got such nice vibrato.

snniifff

I've been hunting all daaaaaaay and this door blocks my waaaaaaaay. Sister, won't you let me iiiiiiiiiiiiiin.
Haha! See?

No one could copy that!

Now let's eat before this hare goes cold.

The following day, Demane prepared to hunt for their next meal.
Alright then.
This door doesn't open until you hear my singing.

"*Sounds*" like a plan.
heheh
Guh, you and your puuuuns...
SMAK

Let's see *you* come up with a better one!
♫
CLUNK
TUP
TUP
TUP
shiver
sshhhhhhh

skrch
skrch

The day passed by, and it started to get dark.
Get over here you pesky ashes.
Back under the pot with you!
SHUFF
SHUFF
SCRUFF

"I'VE BEEN HUNTING ALL DAAAAAAAY, AND THIS DOOR BLOCKS MY WAAAAAAAAY. SISTER, WON'T YOU LET ME IIIIIIIIIIIIN."

Okaaaaaaay!

I'll just let you right in-

NOT!

Alright, bozo!
I don't know who you think you are, but that's **not** my brother's voice.

So you're not getting in here, you got that!? ***SCRAM!***

...
TOO ROUGH...
YOUNGER VOICE...

YOUNGER VOICE...

CRACK

HEAT
SOOTHES THE VOICE.
FOOOM
CRAK

SOOTHES.
SSSSSS.
SSS

SSSS
CRACK

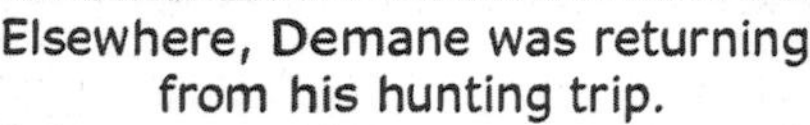
Elsewhere, Demane was returning from his hunting trip.

"So, Demazana, I know you enjoyed the hare yesterday."

"Well, I couldn't find any hares, so I had to go with..."

"PLAN BEE!"
Get it? I got us bees.
ZZ ZZZ
BZZZ ZZZZ

sigh Hopefully her love of puns will distract her from the hunger.
SLUMP
Not much meat on bees, y'know.

CRACK

Hmm?

Looks like something had better luck hunting than I did...
BZZZZZ

Man, whatever it was, it went all-out eating this thing. Dug its teeth right into the bone.

... human teeth?

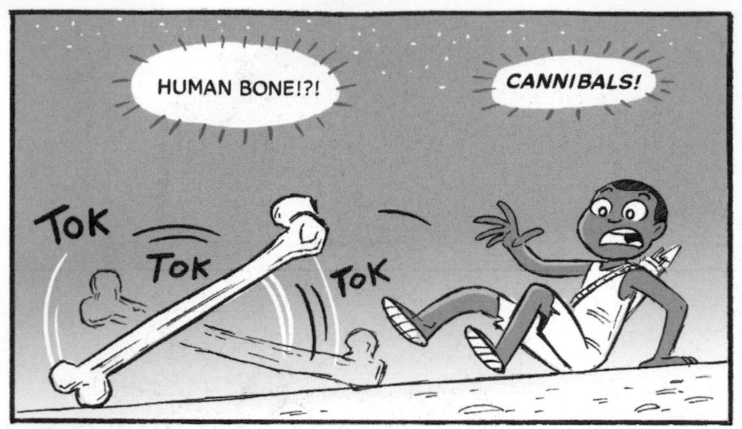
HUMAN BONE!?!
CANNIBALS!
TOK
TOK
TOK

And not far from the house!
I gotta get back to Demazana!

TUD TUD TUD TUD

TUD TUD TUD TUD

POKE
POKE

I've been hunting all daaaaaaay and this door blocks my waaaaaaaay. Sister, won't you let me iiiiiiiiiiiiiiin.

Okaaaaaay!

Thank goodness you're back!

Earlier there was someone...
SHFFF

I've (huff) been hunting-
-all daaaaaaay

And this door blocks (huff)
my waaaaaaaay.

Sister, won't you...

Demazana!!!!!

Dema...
...zana.

We should never have left home...

We should have just tolerated the hitting and the hunger...
Anything would have been better than this!

PEFF

Ashes...

SHFT

TUP TUP TUP

SNP
SHFFF

snff

snffle

Demazana!
Oh! Demane!

You found me!

C'mon, let's get out of here-
No, wait!

He's fast and he's clever, if we leave he'll just chase right after us.

We have to keep him off our trail, at least until we can get back to the cave.

I think I've got just the thing.
SNAP

FLAP

RUSTLE

ZAH!
SHE BITES-

SHFFF

BZZZZZ
BZZZZZZZZZ
BEES!

BZZZZZZZ
AAAAAA
BZZZZZZZZZZZ

AAAAAAAAAAAAA
BZZZZZ
SPLASH

BZZZZZZ
AAAAAAAAA
BZZZZZZZZ

Heh, good thing we had a Plan Bee, huh? Huh?
Are you serious?! I came up with that one when I got the bees.
I didn't hear you say it.

Let me just grab my spears and we're out of here.

Maybe there's some honey inside this-

SPARKLE

What's he got back here?
Wait, that might not be a good-

SHHFFF

GASP!

gleeeam
GLINT

Well, if a run-in with a cannibal and coming out rich is the worst thing to happen out here...
I'd say we're doing all right so far.
Yeah! But let's try not to make a habit out of this.
The End

"HYENA AND JACKAL"
BY CHRIS SCHWEIZER
...SO THEN JACKAL AND HYENA WENT TO BED, BUT JACKAL ONLY **PRETENDED** TO SLEEP.

WHEN MASTER SLEPT ALSO, JACKAL SMEARED FAT ON HYENA'S TAIL, AND THEN ATE ALL THE REST THAT WAS IN THE HOUSE!
AND WHEN THE MASTER AWOKE, HE BLAMED **HYENA**, 'CAUSE HE HAD FAT ON HIS TAIL.
EVIDENCE.

YOU KNOW THIS ONE?
DON'T HAVE TO **KNOW** IT TO KNOW HOW IT COMES OUT.
JACKAL **ALWAYS** CAUSES MISFORTUNE, AND NEARLY ALWAYS GETS **AWAY** WITH IT.

I **LIKE** JACKAL.
YOU **WOULD,** WITH YOUR LOADED DICE.
HEY!

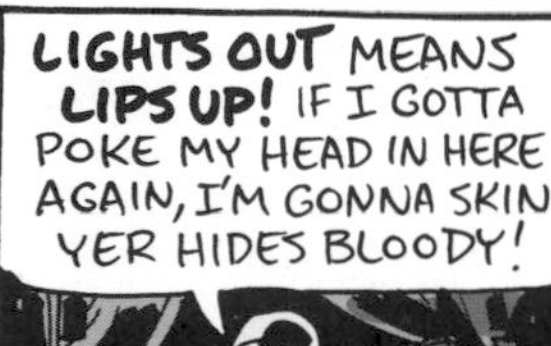
LIGHTS OUT MEANS **LIPS UP!** IF I GOTTA POKE MY HEAD IN HERE AGAIN, I'M GONNA SKIN YER HIDES BLOODY!

PSST! KEFU!
WHAT?

BARUTI'S STORY GAVE ME AN IDEA!

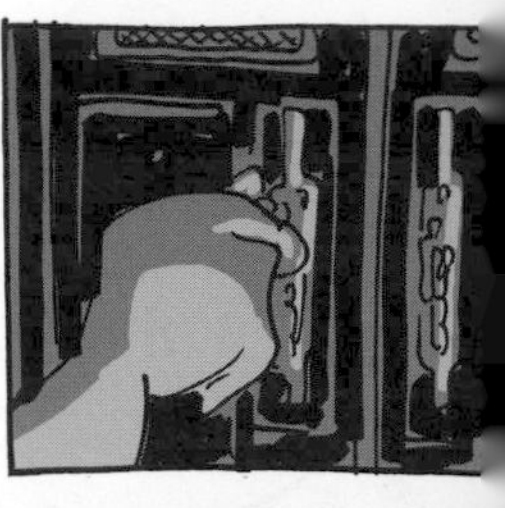

THE OFFICER'S LIQUOR? WE'LL GET LOCKED UP FOR A YEAR IF WE GET CAUGHT TAKIN' THAT!
WE WON'T GET CAUGHT. WE'LL POUR SOME ON BARUTI'S CLOTHES AND THE SERGEANT WILL BLAME **HIM**!

HEE HEE!
SHH!

GLUG GLUG
AAAAGH!

WHAT'S ALL THIS NOI-

Y'KNOW, I **REALLY** HATE THOSE JACKAL STORIES.
END

"SNAKE AND FROG NEVER PLAY TOGETHER"
CSM 2013
I'VE TOLD ONE TALE, I'LL TELL ANOTHER. CALL YOUR SISTER, CALL YOUR BROTHER!
HEAR NOW WHY...
MAMA FROG HAD A CHILD.
MAMA SNAKE HAD A CHILD TOO.
ONE MORNING THEY BOTH RAN OUT TO PLAY.
MAMA SNAKE TOLD HER DAUGHTER:
WATCH OUT FOR THINGS WITH CLAWS THAT CATCH AND TEETH THAT GNAW! DON'T GET LOST, AND BE BACK BEFORE DARK!
MAMA FROG TOLD **HER** DAUGHTER:
WATCH OUT FOR THINGS THAT PECK OR BITE! DON'T FIGHT, AND GET BACK BEFORE SUNDOWN!

CLAWS AN'GNAWS, CLAWS AN'GNAWS, WATCH OUT FOR THE CLAWSAN'GNAWS
SKIP SKIP
OOOF!
FUMP!
WHO ARE YOU? ARE YOU A PECK-OR-BITE?
WHATEVER THAT IS, NO! MY MAMA CALLS ME "SNAKEGIRL!" ARE YOU A CLAWSAN'GNAWS?
O'COURSE NOT, YOU CAN SEE I'M NOT! MY MAMA CALLS ME "FROGCHILD!"
STAAAARE

YOU DON'T LOOK ANYTHING LIKE ME!
SMACK! SMACK!
YOU WISH A WISH, I'LL WISH A WISH TOO!
MAY YOUR WISH AND MY WISH BOTH COME TRUE!

ALONG-ABOUT DARK THEY BOTH WENT HOME —
FROGCHILD! WHAT ARE YOU DOING, CLIMBING ALL OVER LIKE THAT??
I'M SLITHERING! MY NEW FRIEND TAUGHT ME HOW!
SLITHERING? WHAT NEW FRIEND TAUGHT YOU THAT?
HER NAME IS SNAKEGIRL, MAMA!

LISTEN CAREFULLY, DAUGHTER, TO WHAT I SAY NOW.

SNAKE COMES FROM A BAD FAMILY. THEY ARE BAD PEOPLE!

KEEP AWAY FROM THEM! THEY HIDE POISON IN THEIR TONGUES, THEY'LL CRUSH YOU WITH THEIR HUGS!

THEY'LL **EAT** YOU!

I'M HUNGRY, MA!
EH EH! STOP THAT, WHAT A SIGHT YOU ARE!
STOP THAT CRAZY LEAPING! YOU'LL BREAK EVERY BONE IN YOUR BACK! WHO TAUGHT YOU TO DO THAT?
OH, HER NAME'S FROGCHILD! TRY IT, MAMA, IT'S FUN!
FROG, CHILD? DID YOU SAY "FROG," CHILD?
YES, SHE'S MY NEW BEST FRIEND!
IS SHE, NOW! YOU MEAN TO TELL ME YOU PLAYED ALL DAY WITH A FROG AND STILL CAME HOME HUNGRY?
OH, SHE WAS HUNGRY TOO, AFTER SHE LEARNED THE SNAKE-SLITHER GAME!
I'LL BET SHE WAS!
WELL, CURL UP CLOSE, CHILD, AND LET ME TELL YOU ABOUT A NEW GAME!

...PLAY ALL YOU LIKE, BE HOME BEFORE DARK!
CLAWSAN'GNAWS, CLAWSAN'GNAWS—
YOUR WISH AN' MY WISH, EVER COME TRUE!
FRO—OOG-CHILD!
?
ANYBODY HO-OOME?
JUST ME, FROGCHILD!
THERE YOU ARE! COME OUT! LET'S PLAY!
NO, I CAN'T, MY MAMA'S OUT, AND SHE TOLD ME TO STAY IN THE HOUSE!

AW! WELL, YOU LET ME IN, AND WE'LL PLAY INSIDE!

NO, I CAN'T, MAMA SAID DON'T!

BUT I WAITED ALL MORNING FOR YOU!
MY MAMA TAUGHT ME A NEW GAME!
I WANT TO TEACH IT TO YOU!

I BET YOU DO.
OH, YOU DON'T KNOW WHAT YOU'RE MISSING!

GROOOWWL

BUT I DO KNOW WHAT YOU'RE MISSING!

HA HA HA HA!
HA HA HA HA!
WELL...
GOOD-BYE, FROG!
FROG AND SNAKE HAVE A WAY OF SITTING VERY STILL, LOST IN THOUGHT, FOR HOURS.
DO THEY THINK ABOUT THE DAY THEY WERE FRIENDS?
DO THEY WONDER WHAT WOULD HAVE HAPPENED IF NOBODY'D SAID ANYTHING?
MAYBE THEY DO; MAY YOUR WISH AND MY WISH SOMEDAY COME TRUE!
ADAPTED FROM ASHLEY BRYAN'S "AFRICAN TALES, UH-HUH"
CSM '13

Why Turtles Live In Water
A TALE FROM WEST AFRICA
ART BY
JARRETT WILLIAMS

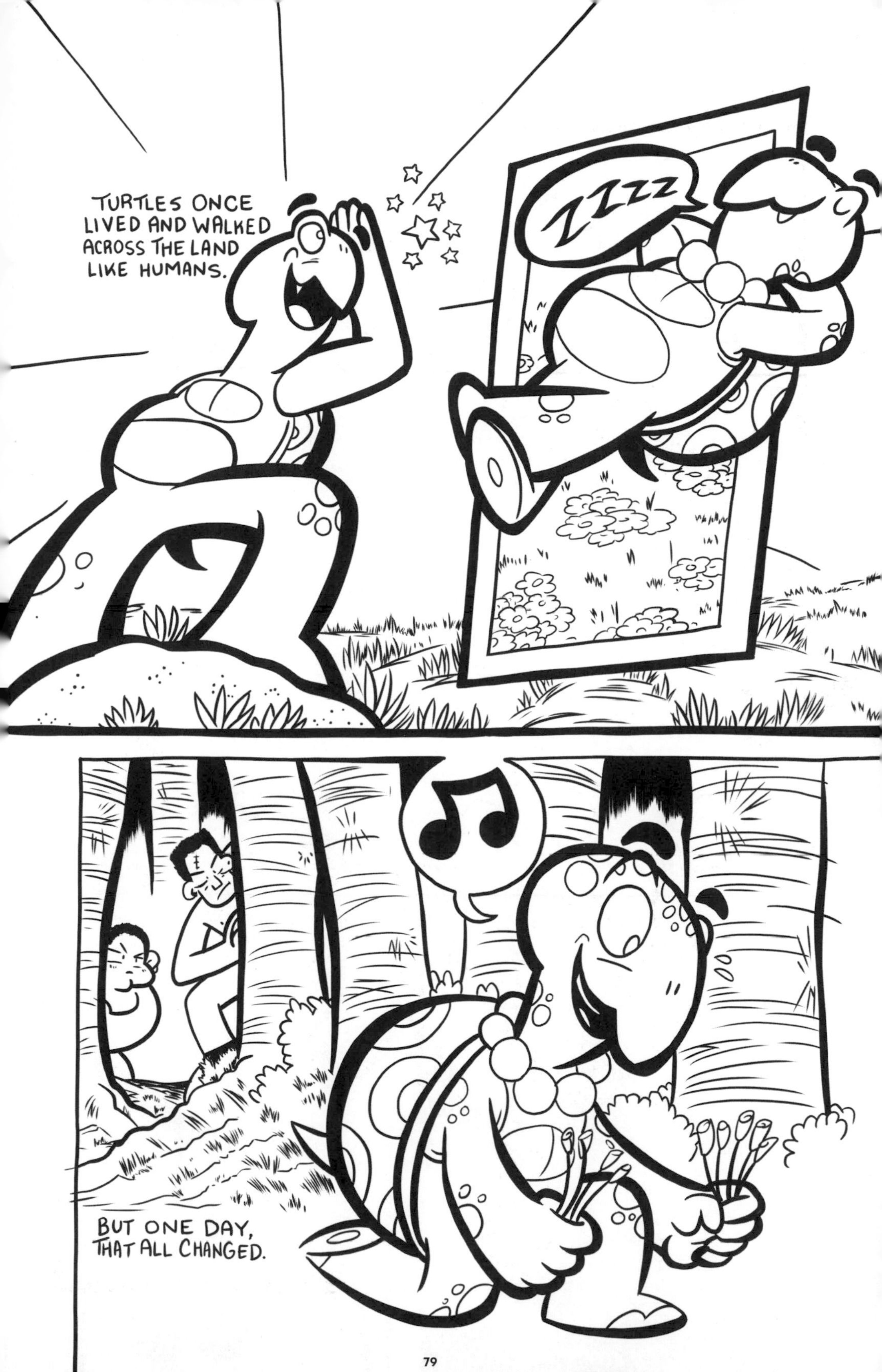
TURTLES ONCE LIVED AND WALKED ACROSS THE LAND LIKE HUMANS.
ZZZZ
BUT ONE DAY, THAT ALL CHANGED.

Sneak
Sneak

YUM!

THE SHADY HUNTERS BROUGHT THE TURTLE TO THEIR VILLAGE...

..AND IN FRONT OF THEIR CHIEF.

GOOD JOB, YOU TWO.

HOW SHALL WE **COOK** HIM?

THAT'LL NEVER WORK! WHY DON'T YOU THROW ME IN THE WATER AND DROWN ME?!
EXCELLENT IDEA.
TOSS!
SPLASH!!!!
PREPARE THE POT.
?!

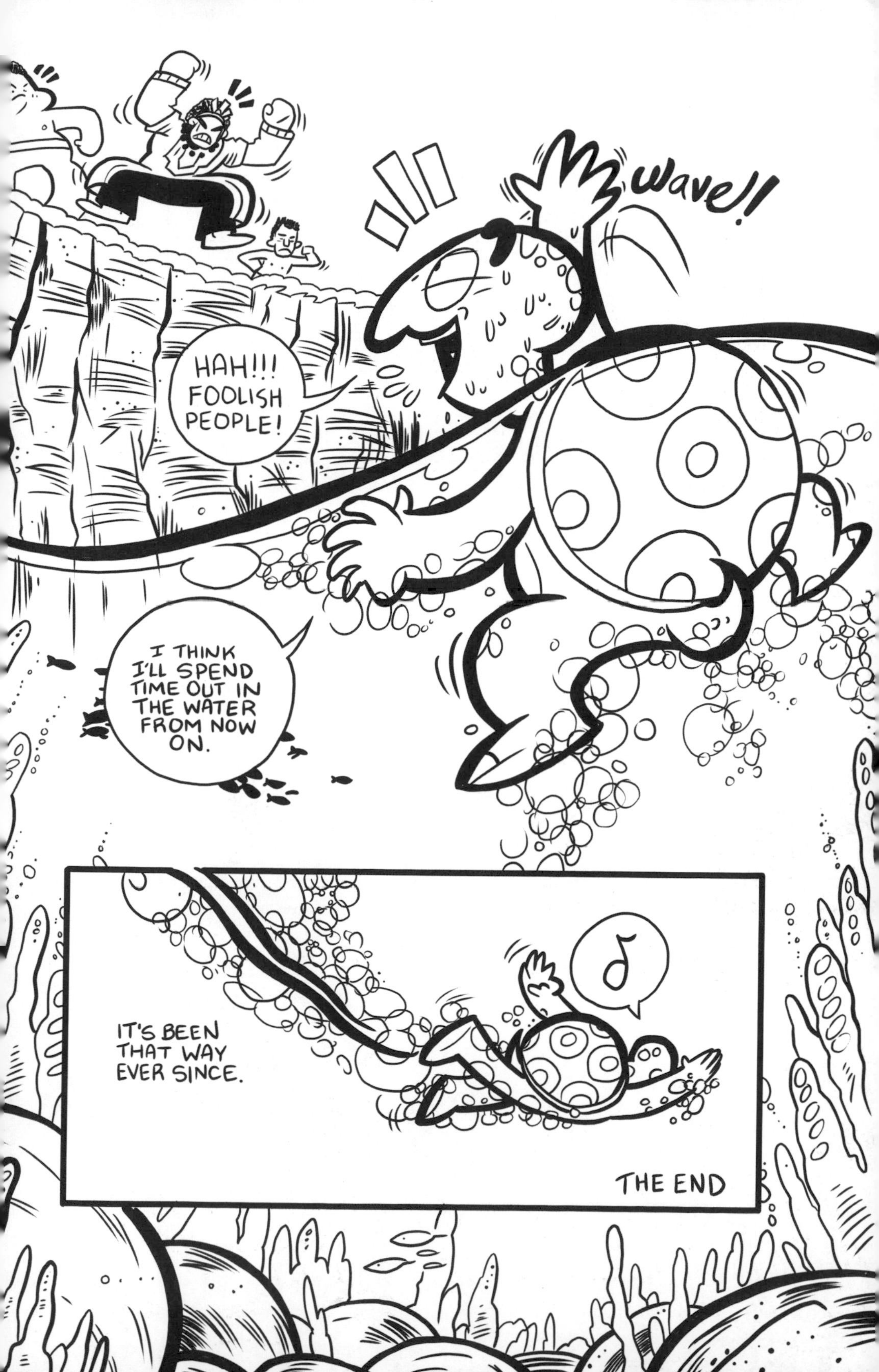
wave!!
HAH!!! FOOLISH PEOPLE!
I THINK I'LL SPEND TIME OUT IN THE WATER FROM NOW ON.
IT'S BEEN THAT WAY EVER SINCE.
THE END

THE STORY OF THE THUNDER AND THE LIGHTNING

Adapted by Kate Ashwin

CRRASSH!

ONCE, THERE WAS A SHEEP FARM.

ON THAT FARM LIVED A FAMILY.

A FAMILY WITH A PROBLEM.

THE FARMERS' DAUGHTER, **THUNDER**, WAS A HARD-WORKING WOMAN...
Wooooo hooooo!
BUT HER SON, **LIGHTNING**, WAS SOMETHING ENTIRELY DIFFERENT.
HE LOVED NOTHING MORE THAN TO DESTROY THINGS, AND NO MATTER HOW MUCH HIS MOTHER SHOUTED-
-AND SHE DID, INDEED, **SHOUT**...
LIGHTNING!
LIGHTNING AND HIS DESTRUCTION COULD NOT BE CONTAINED.
CRRAAASSH
STOP THAT RIGHT NOW!
SMASH!!
CRUNCH!
meeeh?

FINALLY, THE FARMERS COULD TAKE NO MORE.
Good news, dear!
We've bought you a house in town!
Oh! That's wonderful!
When can we move in?
NOW!
CONGRATULATIONS ON LEAVING
YOUR NEW HOUSE

DESPITE HER STRONG SUSPICION THAT SHE'D BEEN EVICTED, THUNDER SETTLED INTO TOWN LIFE PERFECTLY.

BUT AS LIGHTNING GREW OLDER, HIS BEHAVIOR GREW **WORSE**.

CRRAAASH!

Who broke my window?

NNNNNRRRRRRRRRRRRRR LIGHTNING!

EVEN THE OTHER CHILDREN DIDN'T KNOW WHAT TO MAKE OF HIM.
It's that WEIRD kid!
He breaks everything!
Didn't he release all the cows?!
?
Uhm... can I play?
We, uh... don't have room for another.
oh... ok.
What a FREAK!
hahaha!
tsch!
KRRRASH
WHDD!

He really IS a freak!
GET OVER HERE!
LET ME GO!
He could've KILLED us!
Woah!
Did you see that?!

FOR YEARS, THUNDER TRIED HER BEST—

KRRASH!

—TO KEEP THE SON SHE LOVED IN CHECK—

SMASH!

KRSH!

UNTIL ONE NIGHT...
bzzzzz

zzzzz
HEY!
Who let you in here?!

I'LL DESTROY YOU!
zzzz

GET BACK HERE!
zzzzb

LIGHTNING!
What have you DONE?!

COFF!
COFF
COFF!

NNNNNNNN..!
I'm sorry... I did it again, didn't I?
huff.
...It's ok, son.
At least we're both safe.

But... Where can we go now?
plip
plip

PERHAPS I CAN HELP THERE...
I HAVE BEEN WATCHING YOU, MS THUNDER.
YOU TRULY LOVE YOUR SON, DESPITE HIS FLAWS.
...Flaws?
I WISH TO GIVE YOU ANOTHER CHANCE AT PEACE.
Who-?
I AM THE RAIN. AND I HAVE AN OFFER FOR YOU.

YOU MAY LIVE IN THE SKY, WITH ME.
BUT ONLY IF YOU WILL KEEP AN EYE ON YOUR BOY AT ALL TIMES.
SO THEY LEFT FOR THE CLOUDS, TO LIVE WITH THE RAIN. AND WHILE LIGHTNING STILL LOSES CONTROL SOMETIMES...
KRAKK!
BOOM!
HIS MOTHER, THUNDER, IS ALWAYS NEARBY, AND HER SHOUT CAN BE HEARD FAR AND WIDE.
KRAKK!
KA-BOOOM!
AND THAT IS WHY THUNDER ALWAYS FOLLOWS LIGHTNING.

GRATITUDE
A WEST AFRICAN TALE
(LOOSELY) ADAPTED AND ILLUSTRATED BY
D. SHAZZBAA BENNETT
Huff
Huff

...
!

Can I HELP you?

YES PLEASE!!
I'M SO HUNGRY,
dah!

I'M GONNA DIE OF HUNGER!
I THROW MYSELF AT YOUR MERCY, HUNTER.
Okay, don't get all dramatic...

Here you go,
Mister...?

Boaji! I am Boaji the civet!
Thank you, sir! I won't forget it!
Uh-huh.

...

UH.
oh
uh
hey, what's up

Just, y'know, hangin' out...
...
...don't crocodiles belong in the water...?
I got lost, okay!
....
....
Don't laugh.
SIGH
Do you need some help–
Yes! Please!
I'll give you fish in return!
Three big fish!
I like that deal!
Come on, then!

...I'm pretty tired from being lost.
And my feet hurt.
Can't you carry me?
...
No, I can't carry you, so how about this –
I'll tie this rope on and pull you to the river!
See?
OW
Uh, I dunno about this.
Let's...do something els-
OWWWWWWWWW

OOWWWWWWWW

OWWWWWWW

OWW
Oh hey.
Here you are.

Don't forget my fish!
Splsh

Sweet!

!!
...

wade
wade

...

Splsh

....

Seriously, why can't you bring i–
Huh?

YOMP
OW!

OWWWWWWW

AAAAAAAAHHH

OOF.

Look, guys!
I caught a hunter for us to eat!
Come on, everybody!
WHAT?! You little CHEATER!

You-
UH
Now- hang on a minute-!

I saved this crocodile's life!
He was lost in the bush and I helped him find the river!
...
And NOW he wants to eat me!
Is that fair?!

I... I dunno...
Maybe it's not?
But I wanna eat him!

Okay, hunter, we want to be fair.
We'll ask three others what they think.

But who should we ask?
Piranha?
UH
Maybe Lion?

No no no!
You should ask...
um
uhh...

HER!
Old Mare?

Yes! Mare!
Hey, Mare!
Help me!
...

What is the matter?
I saved this crocodile's life, and now he wants to eat me!
Is that fair?

Hmmmm
You are a man.
I know men.

When a mare is young, they build a stall for her.

When she is pregnant, they bring her the best grass –
the best of everything.

...and when she is too old to have foals,
they drive her out,

to fend for herself.

The crocodile would do well to treat you
as your kind have treated *me!*

Yesss!
One vote for us!
woohoo!
....
....

Who should we ask next, hunter?
Ha ha
Ha
Ha
ha
uh
Yeah! You pick again!
Ha ha
ha

Uhhhhhhh

That-
dress!
what

Dress, I helped this lost crocodile find the river.
I saved his life, and now he wants to eat me!
Is that fair?

(Noooo!)
Hear that, guys?
I think she said-
Hmmmmmm

AAHhh!!
...you are a man.
I know men.

When a dress is new, they wear it everywhere.
They accept its beauty as their own

and they say
Aren't
we
lovely?
But it is the dress that is lovely!

And they know it, for they take care of it.
But when it is old, they forget it was beautiful
and throw it in the river.

The crocodile would do well to treat you
as your kind have treated me.
HI-5!
YEAH!

That didn't turn out like I wanted at all!
Looks like everyone agrees with us, hunter!

Wait-!
Get comfy, hunter!

But you still have one more –
–oh!

Boaji! You gotta help me!
Ask him, ask Boaji!!
...?

Oh! I know–
Boaji if you say "I know men"
I swear I will FLIP.
OUT.

No, no.
I know *you.*

What's the matter?
I helped this crocodile find the river – I saved his life!
but he grabbed my leg and dragged me here to eat me!

Is that fair?!
Why bother!
We got 2 out of 3!

We asked two others, and they said it was fair!
But... has anyone heard your side?

...what are you *doing*
Well... no!
No one even asked!

What you need is a judge!
And a fair judge must hear all sides of the argument.
So, if you will agree to accept my ruling, I will hear your case!
Yeah!
I'll tell you what happened!

Judge Hat
What did the hunter do to you, crocodile?
He tied a rope to my foot and dragged me here!
All the way through the bush!

Hmmmm...
IT HURT, OKAY!

No it didn't!
Yeah it did!
You're just a huge baby!
ENOUGH!
I need to see this to be sure.

Crocodile, bring the hunter back to the bank and show me what he did.
Sure!

AND SO...

There.
This is how it was tied?
Yeah.
And this... hurts you?

...After a while it starts to hurt.
HMMMMMMMMM

I'll need to see it to be sure.
wait what
Hunter, show me!

OWWWWWWW
Hmmmm.

And how far was it?
Uh...I dunno, it was pretty far.
...
Then I will need to see that, too.
WHY WOULD YOU NEED TO SEE THAT
HUNTER, SHOW ME!

OWOWOWWWWW

OWWWWWWWWW
Here's where I found him.
Ow.
Wow, This *is* really far from the river...
I told you!!

Well, Crocodile,
I see how the Hunter has hurt you.
You would be right to grab his foot and punish him for it!
Yesss!

Which... you did already,
when you dragged him through the river.
So...

you are even!
That is my ruling.

wait
Come, Hunter.
Leave the crocodile here, so you do not wrong him further.
WAIT-!

HEY!

Thank you, Boaji!
You saved my life!
As you did mine, my friend!

There comes a time when everyone is treated as he has treated others.

END.

THE LION'S WHISKER

HELLO?

COME IN, COME IN.

I HAVEN'T HAD A PROPER VISIT FROM *YOU* SINCE YOU WERE A SMALL CHILD.

TO WHAT DO I OWE YOUR RETURN?

DOCTOR, I... HAVE A PROBLEM, AND I THINK ONLY A POTION CAN FIX IT.

WELL, YOU'VE CERTAINLY COME TO THE RIGHT PLACE.

SIT, AND TELL ME OF YOUR PROBLEM.

IT'S ABOUT... MY HUSBAND.
AND ME.

WHEN OUR MARRIAGE BEGAN, WE WERE SO IN LOVE.
I REMEMBER BEING SO... HAPPY.
BUT THE MORE TIME WENT ON, THE FARTHER WE GREW APART.
NOW, WE BARELY EVEN SPEAK TO EACH OTHER.
WHEN HE COMES HOME FROM THE HUNT, I NEVER KNOW WHAT TO SAY TO HIM.
I CAN NEVER TELL WHAT HE'S THINKING, AND IT SCARES ME.
IT FEELS LIKE WE'RE LEADING SEPARATE LIVES.

I WAS WONDERING IF YOU MIGHT HAVE SOMETHING THAT COULD HELP US RECONNECT.

HMM. BASICALLY, YOU WANT A LOVE POTION?

NORMALLY, I COULD MAKE SOMETHING FOR YOU, BUT I'M FRESH OUT OF A KEY INGREDIENT.
WHAT INGREDIENT? MAYBE I COULD FIND YOU SOME.

A WHISKER, FROM A LIVING LION.

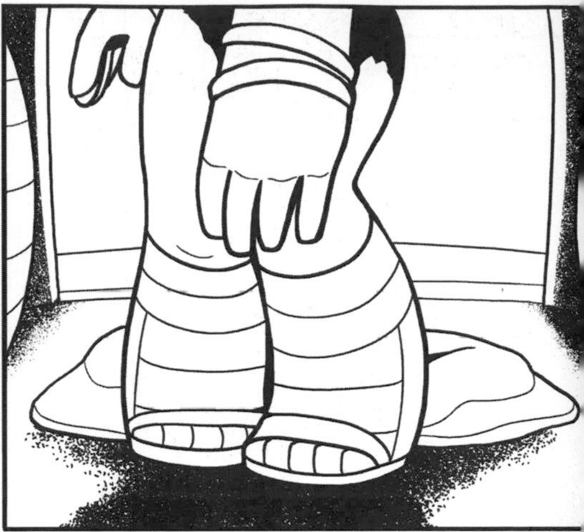

IF THAT'S WHAT IT TAKES, THEN YOU'VE GOT IT.

ONE MONTH LATER.
NOM NOM

MISTER WITCH DOCTOR! MISTER WITCH DOCTOR!
!

I FINALLY GOT IT!

WITH THIS, YOU CAN SAVE MY MARRIAGE, RIGHT!?

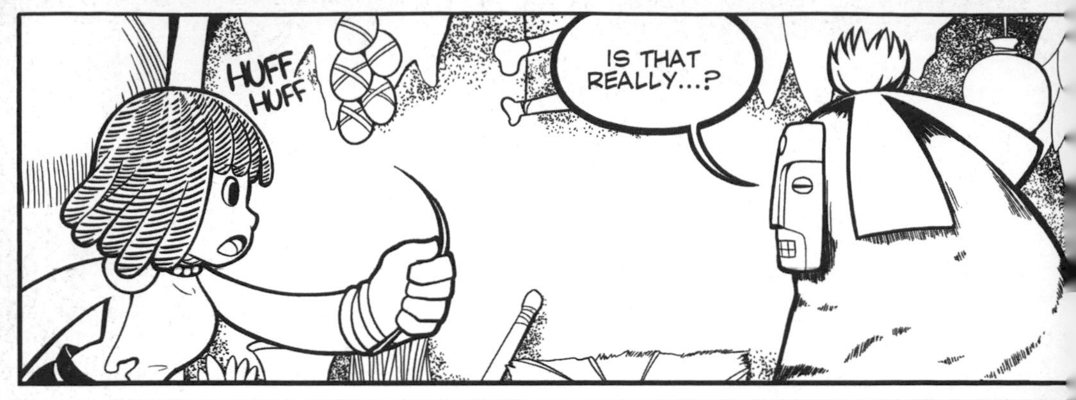
HUFF HUFF
IS THAT REALLY...?

HUFF
SHUFF SHUFF

AMAZING, YOU ACTUALLY GOT ONE!

HUFF
BUT HOW IN THE WORLD DID YOU MANAGE THAT?

IT WASN'T EASY, OBVIOUSLY...
I HEARD THERE WAS A LION WHO WOULD COME TO THE LOCAL STREAM EVERY DAY TO DRINK, SO I DECIDED TO START THERE.

AND SURE ENOUGH...

I DON'T THINK I'VE EVER BEEN SO SCARED.
OBVIOUSLY, I WASN'T ABOUT TO JUST WALK UP AND TRY TO PLUCK OFF ONE OF HIS WHISKERS.
I CAME UP WITH A PLAN --
BUT IT WAS GOING TO TAKE TIME.

CRUNCH
UNCH
CRU

I'M STILL NOT SURE WHETHER HE SAW ME THAT DAY.
BUT I FELT LIKE HE KNEW I WAS THERE.
AND YET, HE LEFT AS SOON AS HE'D EATEN MY OFFERING.
IT SEEMED LIKE MY PLAN MIGHT WORK AFTER ALL.

EVERY DAY, I BROUGHT A PIECE OF MEAT FOR THE LION.

AND EVERY DAY, I WOULD STAND A BIT CLOSER AS HE ATE HIS TREAT.

UNTIL EVENTUALLY...

SNIF SNIFF
NOM
UM... EXCUSE ME...
PLUCK

...AND THEN I RAN AWAY AS FAST AS I COULD.
NOMPH SNOMF
AND, Y'KNOW, CAME BACK HERE.

SO, HOW ABOUT IT?
CAN YOU USE THAT WHISKER TO HELP MAKE MY HUSBAND LOVE ME AGAIN?

• • •

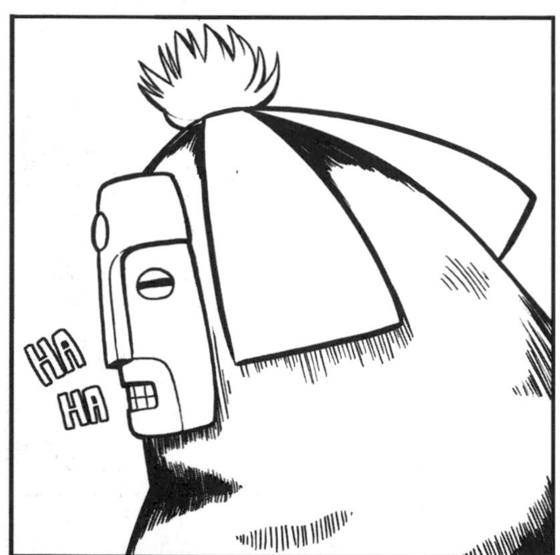
HA HA

W-WHAT'S SO FUNNY?
SNORT

I'M SORRY, IT'S JUST...
WIPE

IS YOUR HUSBAND SO VERY FRIGHTENING?

EH?

CLEARLY YOU UNDERSTAND WHAT IT TAKES TO IMPROVE A RELATIONSHIP.

WITH THE LION, YOU SLOWLY GAINED HIS TRUST WITH PATIENCE AND UNDERSTANDING OF HIS NEEDS.
BUT HAVE YOU EVER TRIED USING THESE METHODS WITH YOUR HUSBAND?

I...
I MEAN, I TRY TO BE A GOOD WIFE TO HIM, BUT IT'S NOT THAT SIMPLE...

IT'S TRUE THAT A MAN'S NEEDS ARE MORE COMPLEX THAN A BEAST'S.
HOWEVER, UNLIKE WITH THE LION, YOU HAVE THE PRIVILEGE OF ASKING YOUR HUSBAND WHAT HIS NEEDS ARE.

I UNDERSTAND THAT OF COURSE, BUT... IT'S SO HARD TO JUST ASK HIM WHAT'S BOTHERING HIM.
IT MAKES ME FEEL LIKE... I'VE LOST SOME KIND OF CONTEST.

IT ALWAYS TAKES BRAVERY TO BE THE FIRST ONE TO ADMIT SOMETHING'S WRONG.

BUT YOU'VE ALREADY PROVEN THAT YOU HAVE THAT IN SPADES.

BUT FOR NOW, KEEP IT AS A REMINDER OF YOUR OWN STRENGTH,

AND OF MY BELIEF THAT YOU CAN SOLVE THIS PROBLEM WITHOUT ANY MAGIC OR TRICKS.

BECAUSE YOU ARE CLEVER AND PATIENT.

AND BECAUSE YOU ARE BRAVE.
END

The greatest of the gods was Ra. Shaper of the sky and the land, ruler of gods and men, cattle and fire, over all creation he ruled.
Isis saw the power of Ra, how he formed life from nothing and could shape worlds from chaos, how his power extended over life and death.
In her heart, she coveted that power.
ISIS AND THE NAME of RA
SCRIPT: CAMERON MORRIS ART: NINA MATSUMOTO

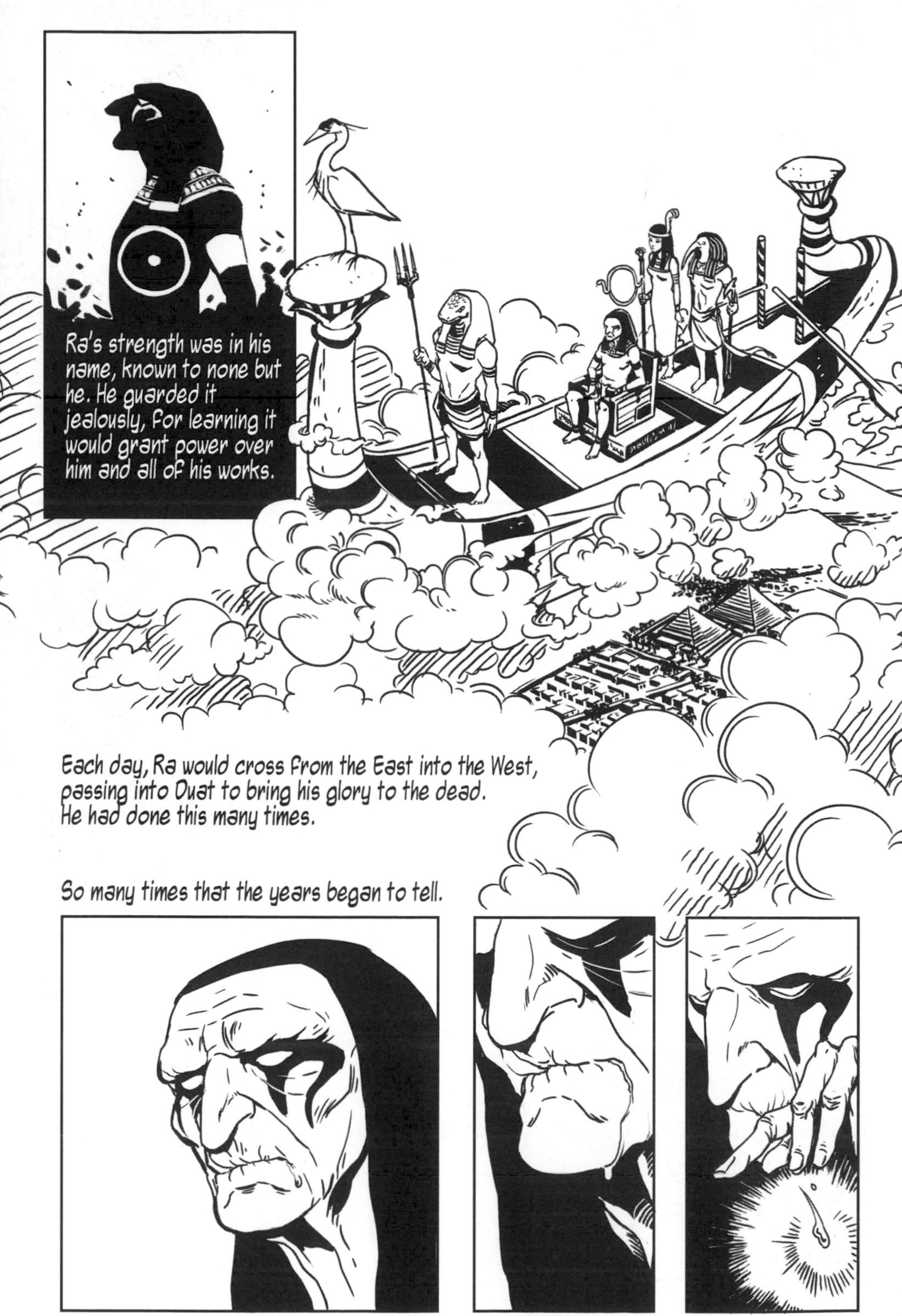
Ra's strength was in his name, known to none but he. He guarded it jealously, for learning it would grant power over him and all of his works.
Each day, Ra would cross from the East into the West, passing into Duat to bring his glory to the dead. He had done this many times.
So many times that the years began to tell.

Isis was the healer,
the goddess of life,
magic and medicine.
Though she had in her the breath of life,
she could not create it from nothing.

But Isis knew that Ra's divine essence was in all of him.
Even in his spittle.
Where the essence dwelled--
--there was life.

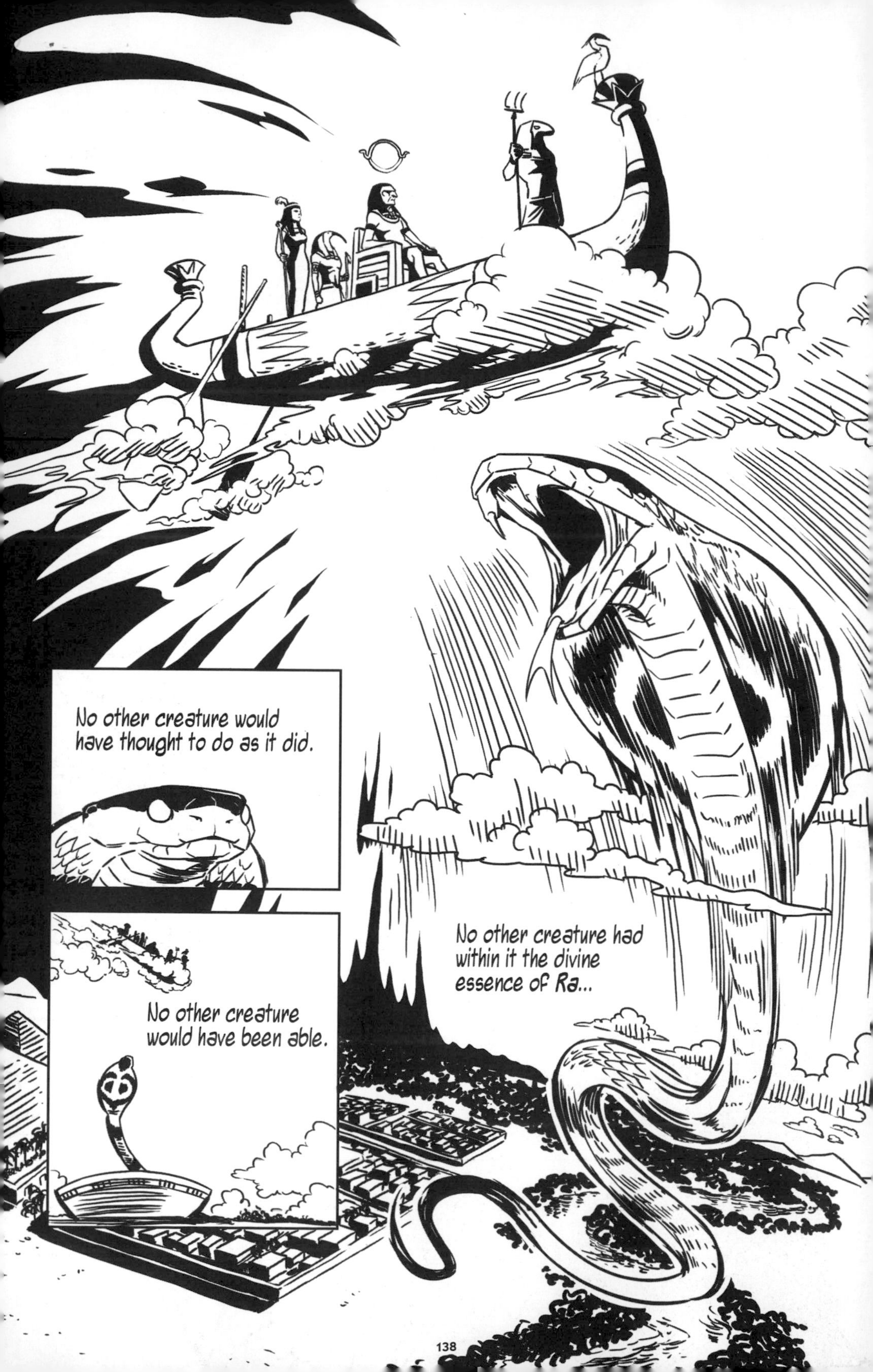
No other creature would have thought to do as it did.
No other creature would have been able.
No other creature had within it the divine essence of Ra...

In every scale and
every drop of venom.

The great god called upon all of his attendants, and all of their arts.
There was no succor for the pain in his bowels.
There was no warmth for the chill in his bones.
There was no quenching the fire that coursed through his veins.
Then he could stand no more.
Isis! Where is Isis? Bring her to me!

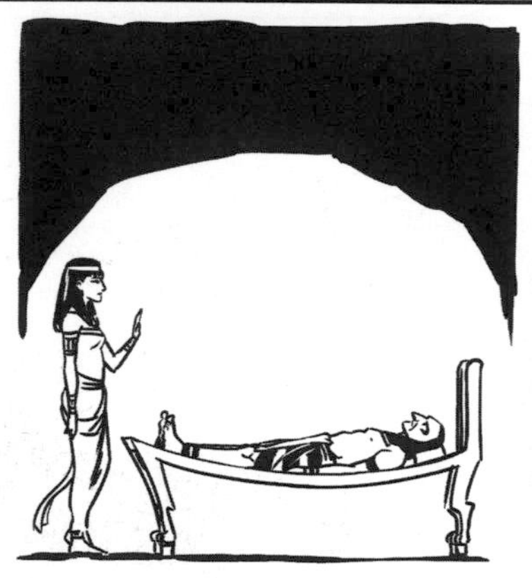

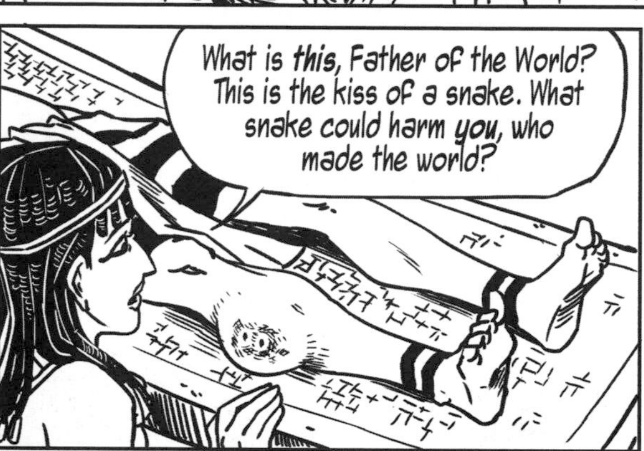
What is *this*, Father of the World? This is the kiss of a snake. What snake could harm *you*, who made the world?

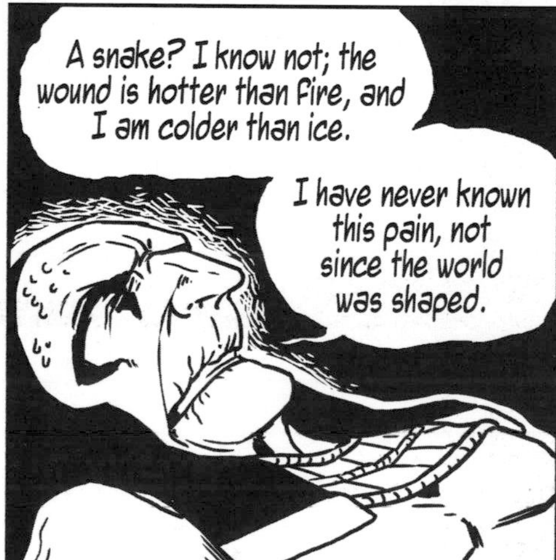
A snake? I know not; the wound is hotter than fire, and I am colder than ice.
I have never known this pain, not since the world was shaped.

Have no fear, Father of the World, for I am the *Mistress of Medicine*, and this poison shall fall to my magic.

I am confounded, O Mighty One, by a power that can harm you and resist me.

Am I to die from this, from a threat I cannot see? Must Ra end so?

No, it need not be so. I can expel this evil, but to do so requires more than my magic. Only by one's name may one be healed of such affliction.

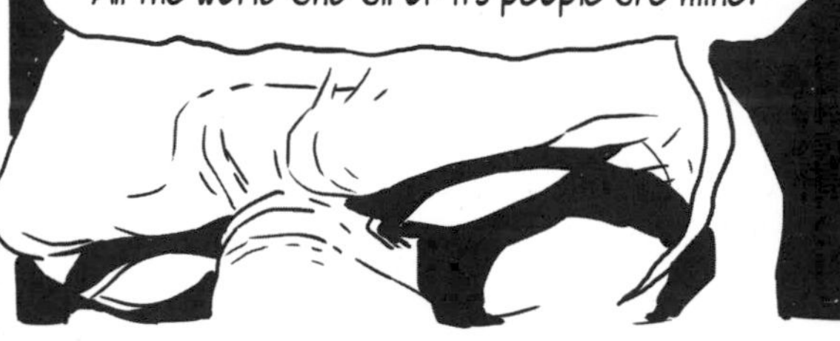
I am known. I am the Shaper, Light giver, Light taker, the Origin from whom all life flows. All the world and all of its people are mine.

In the morning I am Khepri, at noon I am Ra, and at dusk I am Atum.

!!

No. Your **true name**. The secret name, the name you hide from the world. Only by **your** name will you be healed.
Sssso be it!

O Lord, in payment for this I will have a vow. In exchange for your life, swear an oath that your eyes will pass to my son Horus, that the Sun and Moon may be his.
SO I SWEAR.

The Goddess of Medicine spoke the word of power, and the poison was dispelled.
The Father of Heaven was healed.
The payment was made.

That is how Isis, Mistress of the Gods and
first among healers, gained the power over life by a word.
She broke diseases by command, healed the sick,
and the dead did rise at her call.
All praise rose to her, the Great Mother, and it was good.
THE END

Queen Hyena's Funeral
a Yoruba folktale
adapted by
Ma'at Crook
A long time ago in the
Country of the Animals, everyone
got along, even the Flesh-eater
and Plant-eater Communities.

Queen Hyena, Oba, was the ruler of the Flesh-eater Community.

She threw the best parties for all the animals.
She was the best dancer.

She told the best jokes.
HA HA HA HA HA HA HA HA HA HA HA HA HA HA HA HA HA HA
And she never laughed alone.

Respectful and kind, Queen Hyena, Oba, was loved by all.

The Queen worried about her daughter, Princess Hyena, Omoba.

Omoba did not show respect.

She was not kind.

Her dancing was angry.

Her jokes hurt like teeth through flesh.
HA HA
HA
HA HA
HA
She was the only one who found them funny.

On the day the Queen died,
Enough!
We are going to throw a party grander than any Oba had ever thrown.
As your new Queen, I call all my chiefs and elders to make preparations.
I call all animals from all the communities to bring gifts reflecting their love for their late and new Queen.
Go. Now!

On the day of the funeral,

I, Queen Pygmy Hippopotamus, Queen of all Plant-eaters, present a perfect drink of fresh rainwater, never touched by any lips. We grieve your death, Queen Oba.

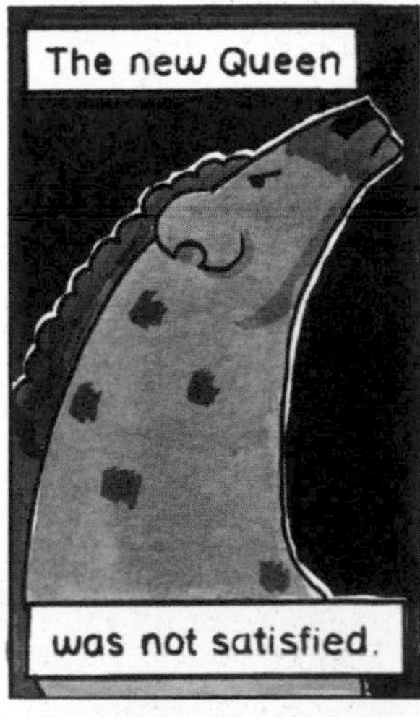
The new Queen
was not satisfied.

The Ant Council lovingly presents this replica of our Queen Oba.

The new Queen
yawn
was not satisfied.

We dance for you, Great Queen Oba.

Oba prized your laughter above any gift.
Today your laughter will roar louder than it ever did in her lifetime.
A hyena walks into a place of worship. The human spiritual leader asks, "Why are you here, Sister Hyena?"
Sister Hyena replies, "To prey."

What's black and white and red all over?
I-I don't know?

Dinner.
LICK

Hey, we better laugh, she is our queen now.
HA HA HA
Right.
HA HA HA HA
HA HA HA

How do you stop a polecat from smelling?
Uh.

You bite their nose off!
gulp.

HA HA HA HA HA HA
HA HA HA
HA HA

The celebration continued.
Great party, our Queen!
It could be better with your help.

We are your subjects, we gladly help. What do you have in mind?
I want to play such a grand joke that a roar of laughter will roll through my kingdom, fit for my mother's funeral.

Soon,

Baby Pygmy Hippo, Queen Hyena would like to meet you.
Me? What an honor.

The Queen is this way, little Chimp.
Oh boy, a visit with the Queen.

Here are the animals you wanted to trick-- I mean, meet.
Not to meet... ...to EAT!
HA HA HA
Eeeeek!
GACK!

Queen Oba wouldn't find this funny!
Rude!
HA HA HA NOM
HA HA HA
Where'd everyone go? What, you can't take a joke?
HA HA HA

From that day to this, hyenas are despised by everyone.

End.

The Girl Who Married a Lion

By Kel McDonald

HAHA
HAHA
HA

Don't be silly. Just go talk to him.

You'll see he's not a lion.

I cannot talk to a lion.

Are you still insisting your brother-in-law is a lion?
Yes. Because he *is*.
You're being stupid.

Look at all the cattle he has. Where would a lion get cattle?

I don't know. But he's definately a lion. I'm sure of it.

Hello, brother.

Hello. Are you all right? You seem upset.

Well, I'm worried about my husband.

He has a strange smell.
WHAT SORT OF SMELL?!
It's a very strange smell.

I can't describe it.

Maybe you can tell me.

SNIFF SNIFF

This is a lion's smell.

What?
It's a LION'S SMELL!

Hmm. We will need a test.

Put a goat outside his home.

No man would eat a goat like that. He is MOST DEFINITELY a lion.

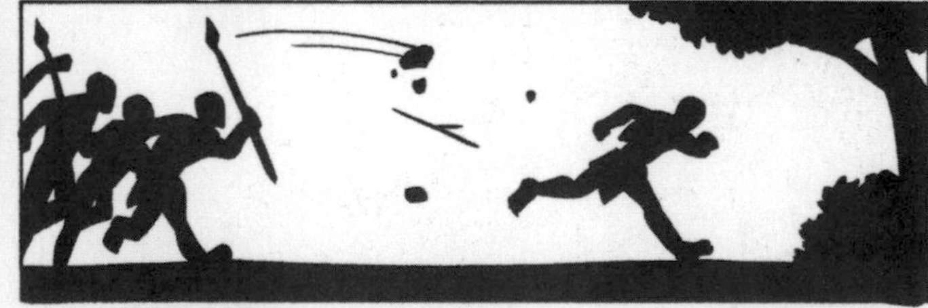

See? He's a lion.

Brother, I'm worried. If my husband is a lion...

Then what are my two sons?

We will have to test the boys in a special way.

I am testing this cage.
Get in.

I want to see if it is strong enough to give protection against lions. I will come back tonight and see if the lions have managed to break it.

Don't worry. Our Uncle would not put us in danger.

This cage must be strong enough to keep the lions out.

SNIFF
SNIFF

RAWR

STAY AWAY FROM THEM!

CONCERNING THE HAWK AND THE OWL
MEREDITH MCCLAREN

WHAT'S THIS?

AN OWLET.

FOR SERVICE TO THE KING, MY EFFORTS ARE REWARDED.

AND HE HAS PERMITTED ME TO CHOOSE A PREY OF MY LIKING, TO ENJOY WITHOUT REPERCUSSION OR REPROACH FROM HIS COURT.

AND THIS OWLET'S PARENTS? WHAT PROTEST HAVE THEY LODGED?

TAKE IT BACK.
FIND ANOTHER BIRD TO PREY UPON.

THAN THOSE THAT REMAIN SILENT

AND DO THEIR MISCHIEF BY NIGHT.

CHIEF'S HEADS

A TALE FROM ZIMBABWE

DRAWN BY
SLOANE LEONG

THERE WAS ONCE
A MAN OF NOBILITY
WHO HAD TWO BEAUTIFUL
DAUGHTERS.

WHILE TRAVELING, HE HEARD
NEWS THAT A GREAT CHIEF
WAS SEEKING A WIFE.

RETURNING HOME,
HE ASKED HIS DAUGHTERS...

DO EITHER OF YOU
WISH TO PRESENT YOURSELVES
TO BE THE WIFE OF A CHIEF?

THE ELDER DAUGHTER
REPLIED...

YES, I WISH TO BE THE WIFE OF A CHIEF.

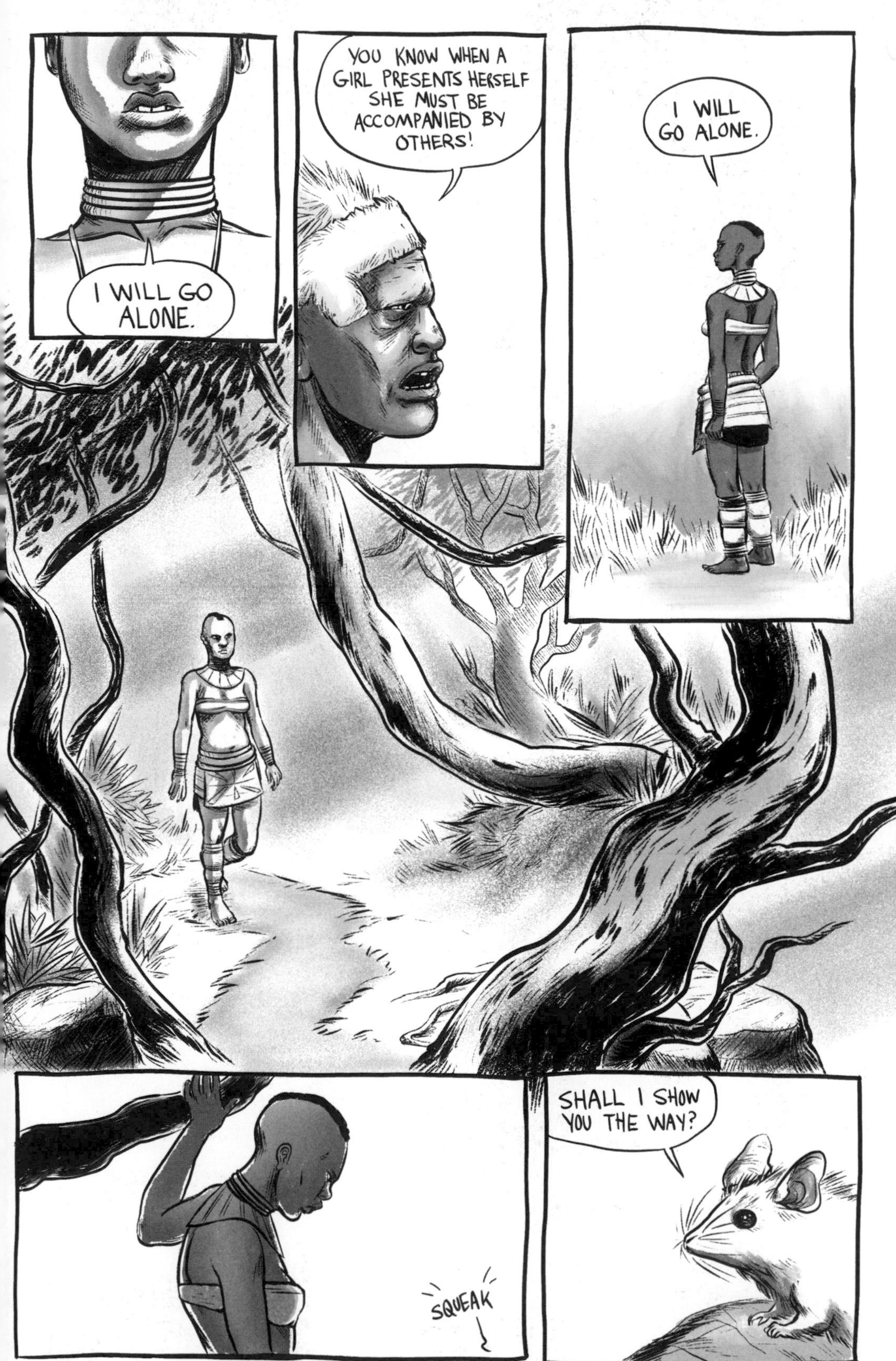
I WILL GO ALONE.
YOU KNOW WHEN A GIRL PRESENTS HERSELF SHE MUST BE ACCOMPANIED BY OTHERS!
I WILL GO ALONE.
SQUEAK
SHALL I SHOW YOU THE WAY?

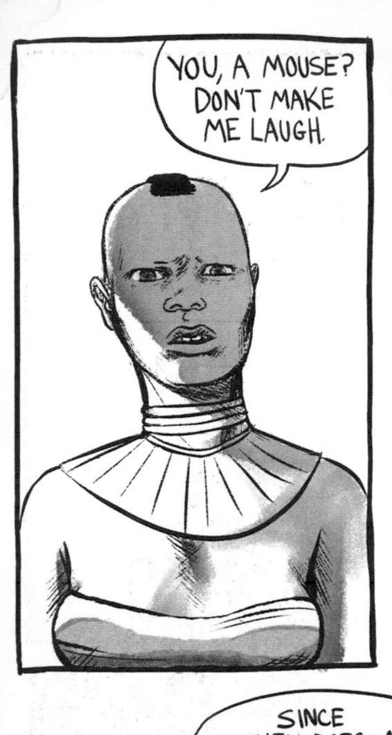
YOU, A MOUSE? DON'T MAKE ME LAUGH.

IF YOU ACT LIKE THIS, YOU WILL NOT SUCCEED.

SINCE WHEN DOES A MOUSE KNOW WHAT SUCCEEDS?

SHALL I SHOW YOU THE WAY?

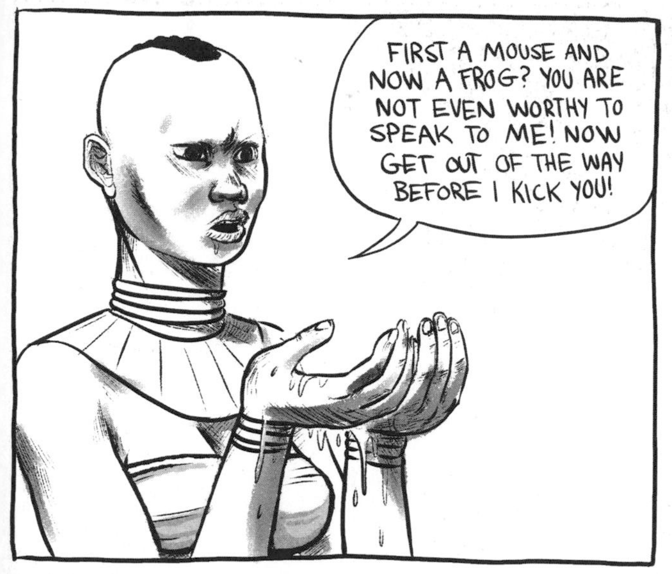
FIRST A MOUSE AND NOW A FROG? YOU ARE NOT EVEN WORTHY TO SPEAK TO ME! NOW GET OUT OF THE WAY BEFORE I KICK YOU!

HAVE IT YOUR WAY, THEN.

PLOP

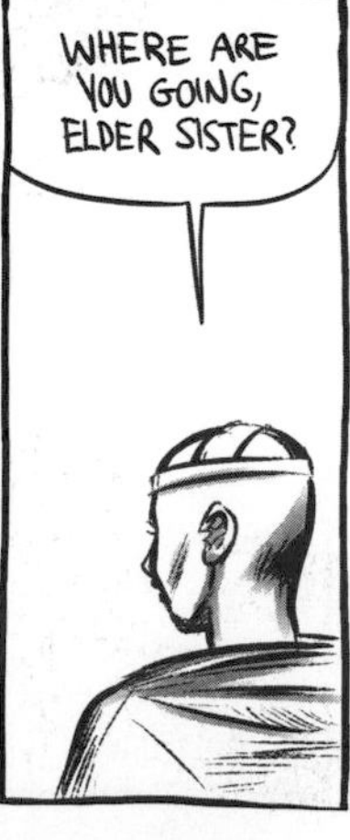
WHERE ARE YOU GOING, ELDER SISTER?

YOU WILL COME UPON TREES THAT WILL LAUGH AT YOU.

DO NOT LAUGH BACK.

YOU WILL SEE A BAG OF MILK.

DO NOT DRINK IT.

YOU WILL MEET A MAN WHO CARRIES HIS HEAD UNDER HIS ARM.

DO NOT TAKE WATER FROM HIM.

YOU OLD HAG!
WHAT NONSENSE.

HA HA HA HA
HA HA HA
HA HA HA
HA HA HA
HA HA HA HA

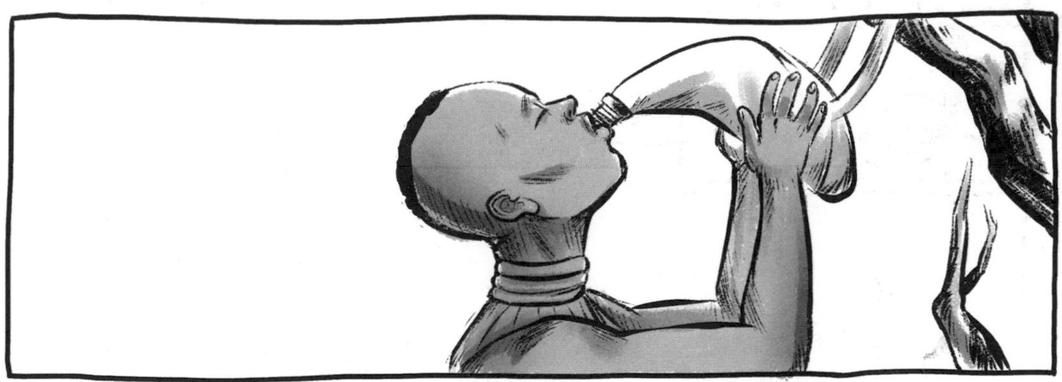

WHERE ARE YOU GOING, SISTER?

WHY DO I OWE YOU AN EXPLANATION? I AM GOING TO BE A CHIEF'S WIFE.

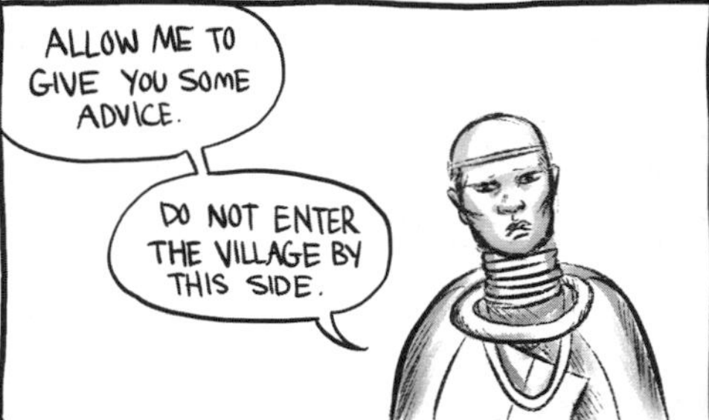
ALLOW ME TO GIVE YOU SOME ADVICE.
DO NOT ENTER THE VILLAGE BY THIS SIDE.

I HAVE COME TO BE WIFE OF THE CHIEF.

WHO HAS SEEN A GIRL COME WITHOUT A BRIDAL PARTY TO BE A BRIDE?

THE CHIEF IS NOT HERE. YOU MUST PREPARE HIS DINNER FOR HIS RETURN.

HMM—
HI
ISSSS
AH!
YOU WILL NOT BE MY WIFE.
GO BACK TO YOUR FAMILY.
HIIISSSSSSS

FATHER, MAY I ALSO PRESENT MYSELF TO BE THE WIFE OF THE CHIEF?

VERY WELL, DAUGHTER.

THE CHIEF CALLED HIS FRIENDS, AND A BRIDAL PARTY WAS PREPARED TO ACCOMPANY THE YOUNGER DAUGHTER.

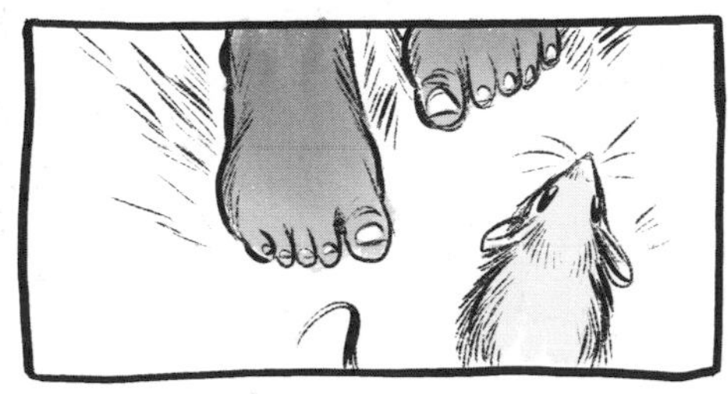

SHALL I SHOW YOU THE ROAD?

IF YOU SHOWED ME THE WAY I WOULD BE GRATEFUL.
!
YOUNG DAUGHTER, WHEN YOU COME TO A BRANCH IN THE PATH YOU MUST TAKE THE LITTLE ONE OR THINGS WILL GO BADLY FOR YOU.
VERY WELL, MOTHER.

THE VILLAGE OF THE CHIEF IS NOT FAR.

YOU WILL MEET A GIRL BY THE RIVER. SPEAK KINDLY TO HER.

THEY WILL GIVE YOU MILLET TO GRIND. GRIND IT WELL.

WHERE ARE YOU GOING?

THIS IS THE END OF MY JOURNEY.

WHY HAVE YOU COME?

I AM HERE WITH MY BRIDAL PARTY TO PRESENT MYSELF TO THE CHIEF.

I SEE. WILL YOU BE AFRAID WHEN YOU SEE MY BROTHER, THE CHIEF?

I WILL NOT BE AFRAID.

YOU MUST PREPARE A MEAL FOR HIM.

HE WILL RETURN TONIGHT.

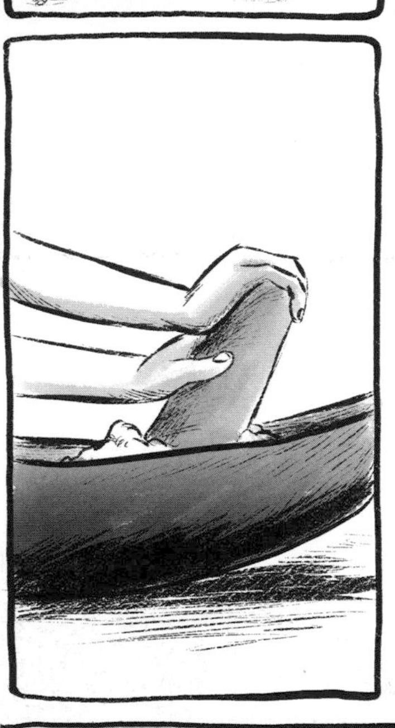

THE YOUNGER DAUGHTER
DID NOT FLEE WHEN THE
CHIEF ENTERED THE HUT.

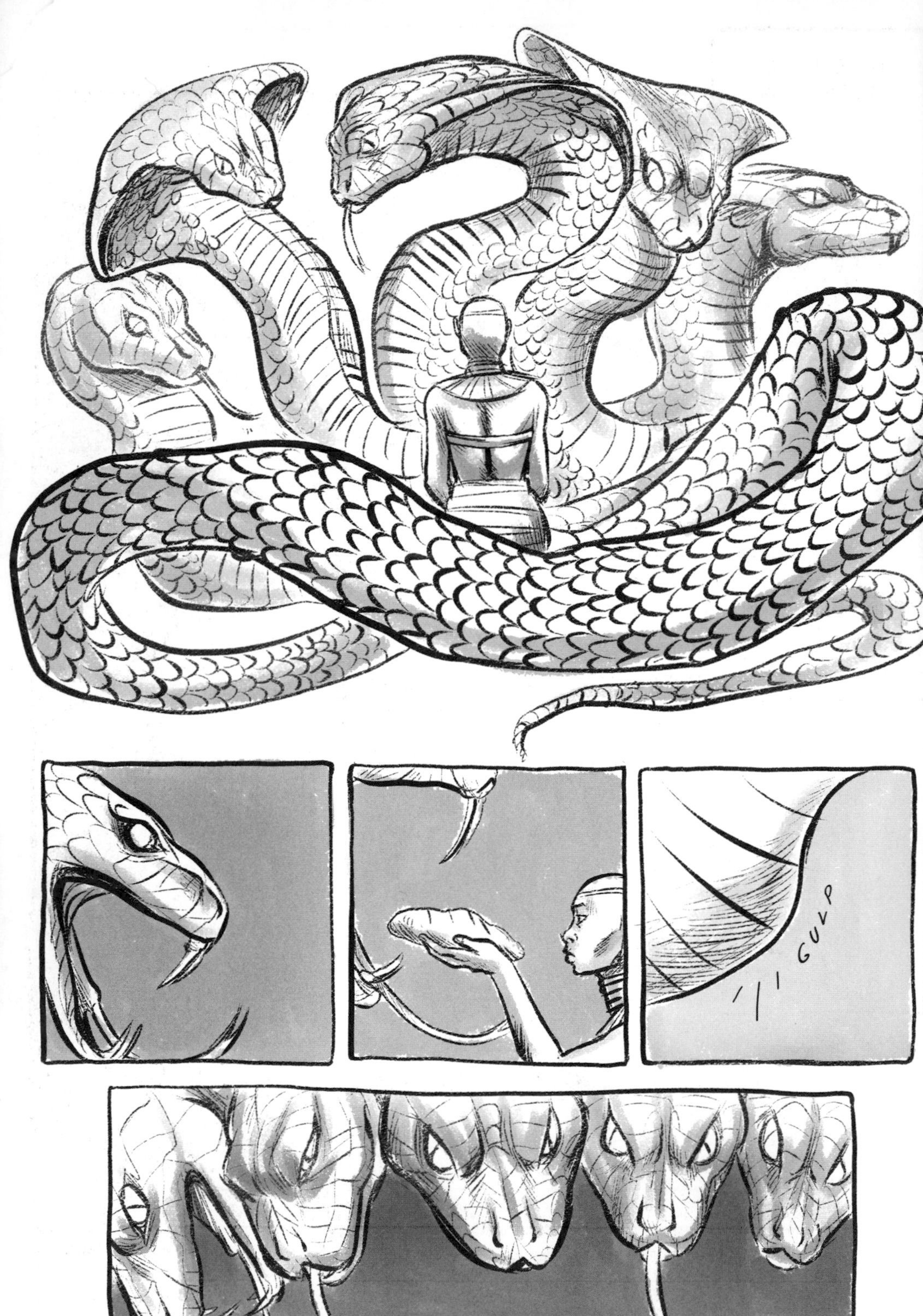

I KNOW WHAT HAPPENS AT ALL TIMES.

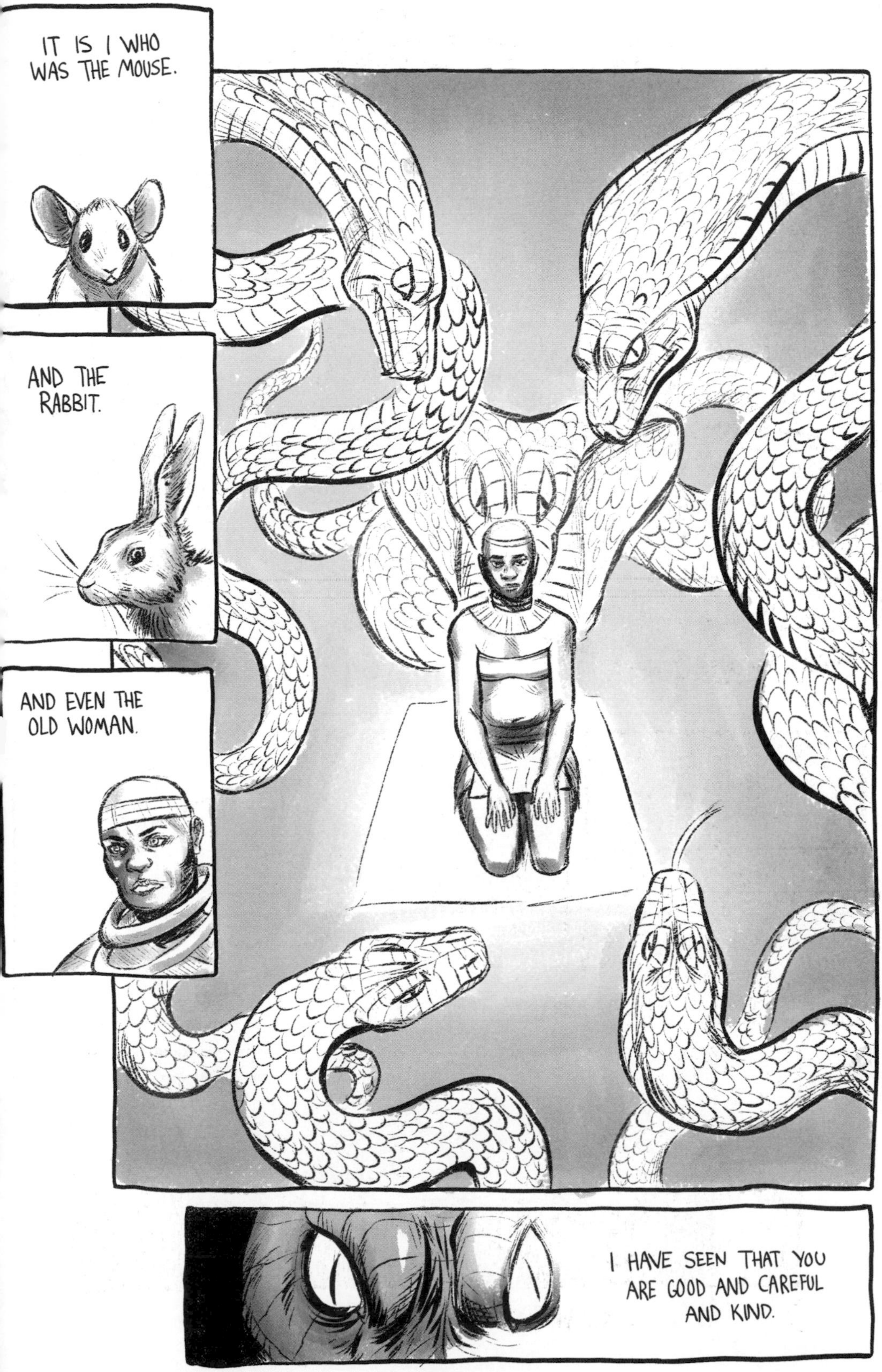

IT IS I WHO WAS THE MOUSE.

AND THE RABBIT.

AND EVEN THE OLD WOMAN.

I HAVE SEEN THAT YOU ARE GOOD AND CAREFUL AND KIND.

WILL YOU BE
MY WIFE?

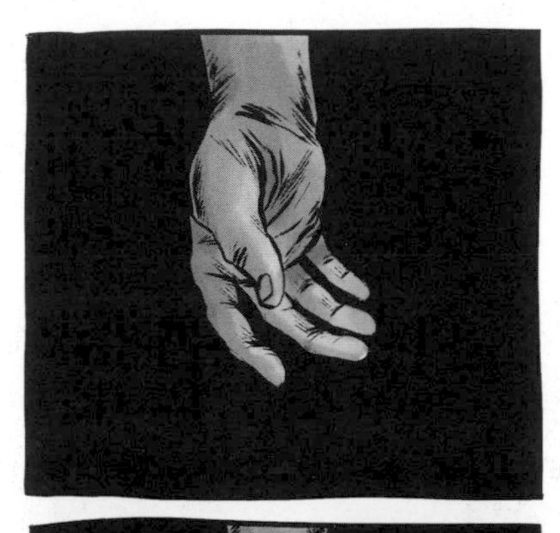

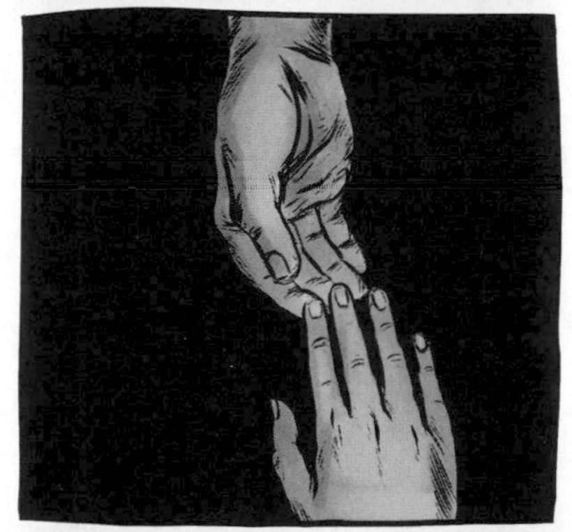

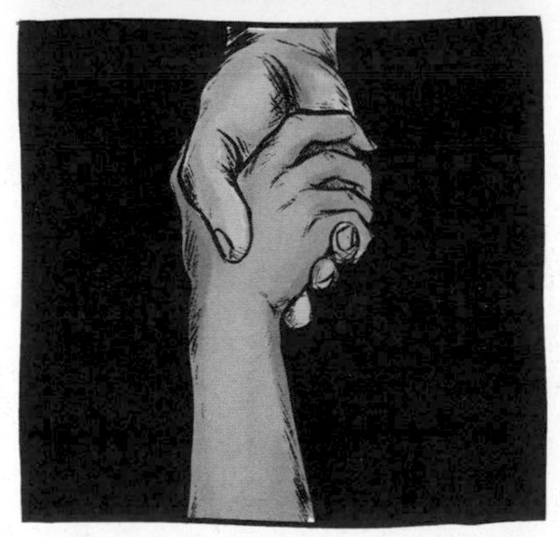

The Stranger
by
Faith
Erin
Hicks

PEOPLE OF **FACTION CALABAR**, TONIGHT WE CELEBRATE OUR PAST CONQUESTS, AND LOOK FORWARD TO GREATER VICTORIES!

I DO NOT KNOW YOU.

MY NAME IS OYAIKEN, SIR. I PREPARED THE FOOD FOR THIS VICTORY FEAST.
THE FOOD IS WONDERFUL, OYAIKEN, BUT IT IS NOTHING COMPARED TO YOUR BEAUTY.

THANK YOU, GENERAL. TO BE TOLD ONE'S BEAUTY SURPASSES THE TASTE OF GOOD FOOD IS A COMPLIMENT INDEED.

HAHAHA! WELL PUT!
I AM A MAN WHO APPRECIATES GOOD FOOD AND BEAUTIFUL WOMEN.

OYAIKEN, I WOULD LIKE YOU TO BRING A DISH OF FOOD YOU HAVE MADE YOURSELF TO MY ROOM TONIGHT.

WEAR SOMETHING A LITTLE MORE ... COMFORTABLE.

IT WOULD BE MY GREAT HONOUR TO DO SO, GENERAL.

INDEED, IT WILL.

OYAIKEN...

YOU LOOK VERY PLEASING TO ME.
THANK YOU, SIR. I HOPE THE FOOD IS JUST AS PLEASING.

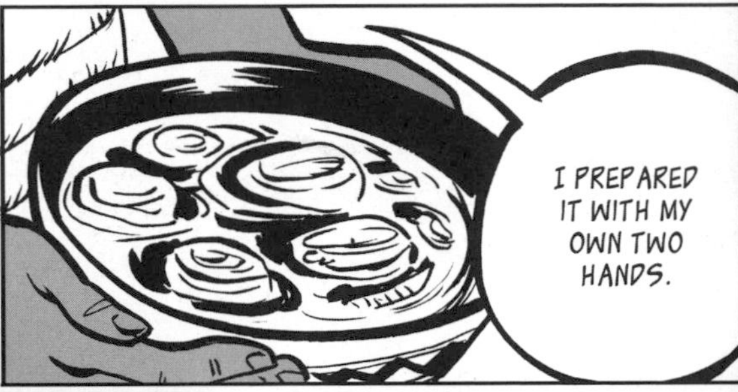
I PREPARED IT WITH MY OWN TWO HANDS.

SLUURRPP

MMM, *DELICIOUS*.

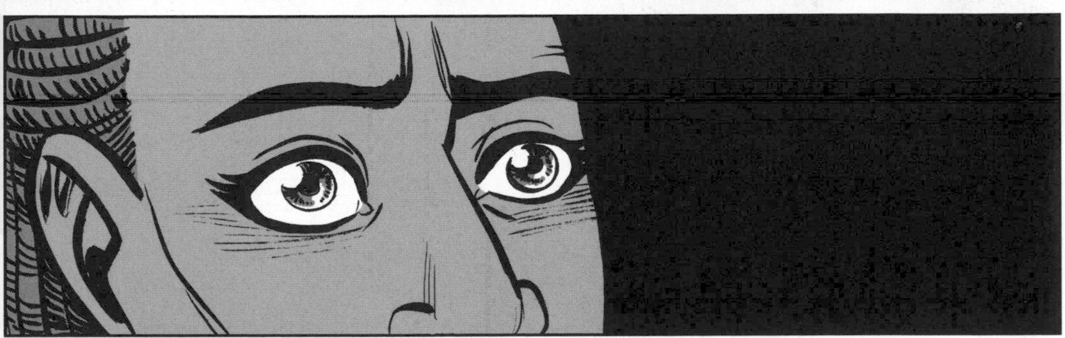

HURRGH

FWUMP

KLAANG

WHAT...
WHAT DID YOU
DO TO ME?

I
POISONED
YOU.
YOU'LL BE
DEAD IN
THREE
MINUTES.

NNOO!
YES.
THIS ACTUALLY
REMINDS ME OF
AN OLD SAYING
MY FACTION
HAS.

"NEVER MARRY A STRANGER,
NO MATTER HOW PRETTY
SHE MAY BE."

WHAT--
WHAT FACTION
ARE YOU--

FACTION
ITU.
SO MUCH FOR
YOUR PLAN TO WIPE
US OFF THE FACE
OF THE GALAXY, HM?
WHUDD

WE KNEW
WE COULD NEVER
DEFEAT YOUR
FACTION USING
FORCE, SO ...
... OTHER
METHODS HAD
TO BE TRIED.

SHURRP

FWUMP

WHAT... ARE YOU?

ISN'T IT OBVIOUS?
I'M A WITCH.

ITU FLEET,
PLEASE RESPOND.

ALL SHIPS
STANDING BY,
SIR.
WHAT ARE
YOUR ORDERS?

ATTACK ALL
SHIPS BELONGING
TO FACTION
CALABAR.
LEAVE
NO ONE
ALIVE.

DO TO THEM
WHAT THEY WOULD
HAVE DONE TO
US.

DEET
DEET

WHO IS
CALLING ME ON
THIS CHANNEL?
THESE LINES ARE
SUPPOSED TO BE
CLEAR FOR BATTLE.

HI MOM. THEY SAID IT WAS OKAY TO CALL.
YOUR ... *THING* ... WENT OKAY?

IT WAS FINE, BABY. IT'S OVER.
TELL ME HOW SCHOOL WAS TODAY.
EH, SCHOOL. SCHOOL WAS SCHOOL. BORING, SAME AS ALWAYS.

YOU GRADUATE NEXT YEAR, HONEY. AFTER THEN YOU'LL BE ABLE TO CHOOSE WHATEVER FUTURE YOU WANT.

I'VE BEEN THINKING ABOUT THAT ... I KNOW YOU REALLY WANTED ME TO STUDY AT THE ACADEMY, BUT I THINK I WANT TO TRAVEL FOR A YEAR ...

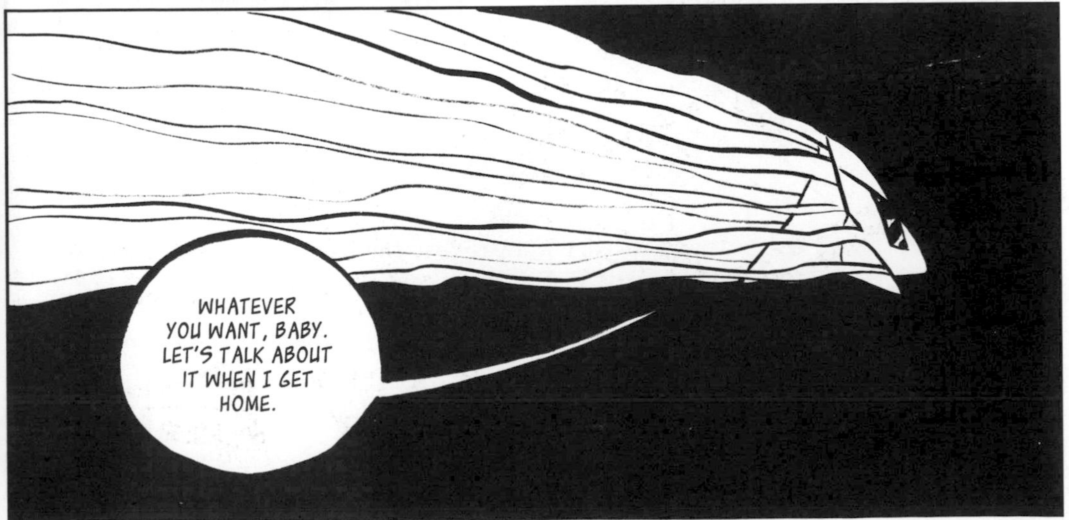
WHATEVER YOU WANT, BABY. LET'S TALK ABOUT IT WHEN I GET HOME.

ABOUT THE ARTISTS

KATE ASHWIN has been writing and drawing online comics for over a decade, and has enjoyed every minute of it so far. Her completed fantasy epic **Darken** can be found online at darkencomic.com, and her ongoing Victorian-era adventure tale, **Widdershins**, at widdershinscomic.com. She lives in the north of England with her husband and loud cats.

D. SHAZZBAA BENNETT is a webcomic artist with a simultaneous love of quirky upbeat stories, cute animals, and Lovecraftian horrors. She's best known for the four-year journal comic **Today Nothing Happened** and currently creates the fantasy webcomic **Runewriters**. All her work can be found at shazzbaa.com!

MARY CAGLE is a comic artist from Texas! She's best known for the autobiographical comic **Let's Speak English**, about her time teaching English in Japan, and also creates the webcomics **Sleepless Domain** and **Kiwi Blitz**. You can check out her work at marycagle.com.

NICOLE CHARTRAND is a concept artist and illustrator hailing from Montreal. She also writes and draws an ongoing fantasy-adventure webcomic, **Fey Winds**. You can find her in close proximity to coffee, and you can find her comic at feywinds.com.

MA'AT CROOK is a writer and artist who was first published in **Womanthology: Heroic**. She grew up wanting to be an artist and veterinarian, so getting to draw a bunch of African animals in **The Girl Who Married a Skull** totally made her inner child climb trees barefoot out of sheer joy. You can keep up with her work by checking out her website, maatcrook.com.

SLOANE LEONG is a Portland-based comic artist and illustrator. She self-publishes her own comics and has drawn and colored things for Image, Dark Horse, Vertigo, and DC. You can find more of her work at sloanesloane.com.

FAITH ERIN HICKS writes and draws too many comics. Previous works include **Demonology 101, The War at Ellsmere, Friends with Boys, Nothing Can Possibly Go Wrong** (with Prudence Shen), **The Last of Us: American Dreams** (with Neil Druckmann), and **The Adventures of Superhero Girl**. She lives in the mysterious Canadian province of Nova Scotia, and can be found online at faitherinhicks.com. Her Twitter and Tumblr are @faitherinhicks.

NINA MATSUMOTO is an Eisner-Award-winning artist who draws **The Simpsons** for Bongo Comics and designs video game t-shirts on the side. She created the OEL manga series **Yokaiden**. She recently illustrated a film poster for a Japanese movie. Her weird pop culture mash-up art can be seen at spacecoyote.com.

MEREDITH MCCLAREN is an illustrator and cartoonist who has no business doing either. Rumor has it she's done work for Oni Press and BOOM! Studios in addition to her own webcomic series, **Hinges**. She may yet do more. Supposedly she has a postal code in Arizona, but really she could be anywhere.

KEL MCDONALD has been working in comics for over a decade—most of that time has been spent on her webcomic **Sorcery 101**. More recently, she organized the **Cautionary Fables & Fairytales** anthology series, while contributing to other anthologies like **Dark Horse Presents** and **Can I Pet Your Werewolf?** She's also worked on **Buffy: The High School Years**. She recently finished a creator-owned series, **Misfits of Avalon**. She's currently working on her self-published series, **The City Between**. Her work can be found at kelmcdonald.com.

CARLA SPEED MCNEIL is best known for her Eisner-Award-winning science fiction series **Finder**, which she writes and draws. Originally from Louisiana, she now lives in Maryland with her husband and two kids, who love folktales. Her story in this book is loosely adapted from the story of the same title collected in Ashley Bryan's wonderful **African Tales, Uh-Huh**. Highly recommended.

CAMERON MORRIS is a part-time short story writer who has previously been published by Cloudscape Comics. He really enjoys the whole comics thing. You can find him at cameronwrites.com.

JOSE PIMIENTA draws most of the time or is having coffee while listening to music. He still lives in the U.S. and likes to walk as often as possible to the beat of a good tune. Most of his comic work is in collaboration with other writers and artists such as Lindsay Durbin, Lauren Affe, Jason Franks, Kel McDonald, and Van Jensen. the-joepi.blogspot.com | rawpads.blogspot.com | sorcery101.net/from-scratch

CHRIS SCHWEIZER is the creator of **The Crogan Adventures** (Oni Press) and **The Creeps** (Abrams). He lives in Madisonville, KY with his wife and daughter. Every once in a while he gets nominated for Eisner Awards but always loses, and he often has a mustache.

KATIE [KTSHY] AND STEVEN [SHAGGY] SHANAHAN are two comic-making siblings who've collaborated on short stories for the **Flight** and **Explorer** anthologies, their own self-published comic **Silly Kingdom**, and the webcomic **Shrub Monkeys**. Katie works as a storyboard artist for animated TV shows, and Shaggy works in video post-production for whatever comes his way. You can catch up with both of them on their websites, ktshy.com and shaggyshan.com.

JARRETT WILLIAMS was born in New Orleans, LA and is 33 years old. He currently lives in Savannah, GA where a majority of his time is spent in his studio pondering life and listening to music from bygone eras. When he's not drawing comics, he's traveling, playing video games, or hanging with friends. He's possibly doing all three at the same time. He created the pro-wrestling/adventure series **Super Pro K.O.!** at Oni Press, and illustrates covers for **Adventure Time** and **Regular Show** at BOOM! Studios.

EXTRAS

Top Right: Concept sketches for Faith Erin Hicks' "The Stranger"

Top Left: Mary Cagle's turn-arounds for her characters

Bottom: Jose Pimienta's designs for all the animals

Top: Katie Shannahan's concept art for "Demane and Demazana"

Bottom: Katie Ashwin's first sketch for "The Thunder and the Lightning"